AN EVIL
NUMBER

AN EVIL NUMBER

To Bev,
scary reading!
Robert Coburn

ROBERT COBURN
A JACK HUNTER MYSTERY

ABSOLUTELY AMAZING eBOOKS

ABSOLUTELY AMAZING eBOOKS

For information contact:
Publisher@AbsolutelyAmazingEbooks.com

ISBN-13: 978-1523289912
ISBN-10: 1523289910

To Molly, a K9 unsurpassed.

OTHER BOOKS BY ROBERT COBURN

A Loose Knot

A Deadly Deception

The Pink Gun

Little Boxes

Bad Tidings

AN EVIL NUMBER

3, 5, 6, 9, 10, 12, 15, 17, 18, 20, 23, 24 ....

A number is called evil if the sum of its binary digits is even.

CHAPTER 1

It had been two months since Martin Hodges died. Sixty days. Sixty was an evil number in the occult charts.

~~~

"Jack, I think I've found you a car," Mike Eaton said excitedly over the phone. "Series 1. Belonged to David Hodges, a music industry biggie. In fact, his kid got killed in a car accident a short while back."

"That wasn't the jerk who ran into the telephone pole on PCH, was it?" Jack Hunter asked.

"Yeah, Martin Hodges. Supposed to have been racing. Cops still looking for the other guy."

"Jesus, that happened right in front of my house," Jack said, stunned. "Three o'clock in the damn morning. No, I didn't know him."

Jack Hunter owned a nice beachfront home just south of the Malibu Colony. He'd leased it out for awhile but had recently moved back in himself. The idea of kicking back and watching the sun settle into the Pacific Ocean was just what the doctor had ordered. Literally.

After a wrenching experience in Key West involving the graves of some children buried in the cemetery there, he had returned to Los Angeles heart sore and his soul desperately in need of healing. A close friend had recommended that he see a psychiatrist. Jack had taken her advice and now seemed to be on the mend.

As a further therapy, and this one of his own making, he'd decided to buy the car of his dreams. A Jaguar XKE, the sexiest thing ever to roll on four wheels. He started looking. Took in a couple of car auctions. But the right one had never come along. Finally, he gave up and turned over the search to Mike Eaton, who specialized in locating and buying classic cars.

"Martin Hodges was supposed to have been a first-class asshole," Eaton said. "Heavy into drugs, kinky sex, all kinds of weird shit. His old man had a few stories going around about himself, too."

"So what's this car like?" Jack asked, getting straight to the point.

"I haven't seen it but I've got pictures," Eaton told him. "Lawyer settling the estate had taken them as part of the inventory. Like I said, it's a Series 1 roadster, triple black. The car's been on blocks in the garage since the old man died back in 1997. Seems his son didn't want anything to do with it. Preferred hot Porsches. Should've learned how to drive one."

"Does the Jag run? Engine could be frozen after all that time."

"From what I've gathered, the car was pampered. Changed the oil on time. Serviced regularly. Always kept inside. Driven only on weekends. The mileage is unbelievably low. But the engine should be okay. Just need to have someone who knows what he's doing to check it over."

"Any idea what they're asking?"

"Does it matter?"

Well, in fact it didn't matter. Jack was quite well off. He'd always had a knack for picking the right stocks. Also, the real estate market in Los Angeles seldom hiccupped, especially when you were talking location, location, location. And location was what Jack's investments there were all about, thanks be given to the smarts of his late ex-wife.

"Be good to have a figure in mind," Jack said.

"Probably looking at sixty grand. Could be higher if it goes to bid."

"When can we see it?"

"I'll set something up for tomorrow morning. The estate is on the north side of Mulholland just west of Benedict Canyon."

CHAPTER 2

The call came in at 0400. Shots fired, man down. Patrol was first on the scene.

Detective Laura Dalton's bedside phone rang an hour later.

"Hello," she answered sleepily, fumbling for the phone and picking up on the third ring.

"This is Rivers. We have a dead body at the Hodges estate."

Jason Rivers was the new man at the Van Nuys Division of the Los Angeles Police Department. Following graduation from the Academy, he'd spent a year on patrol and then was fast-tracked to detectives winding up on the homicide table. His quick advancement had been met with resentment by some of the older officers.

"Give me a minute," Dalton grumbled, sitting on the side of the bed. "Now, explain why you are calling me?"

"Well, er, shouldn't I?"

Duty rotation had given Rivers the detective-on-call assignment for the night shift. Usually that officer handled all calls requiring a detective's presence unless there were multiple homicides or a high-profile case, such as with O. J. Simpson. Then they'd call out the big guns. Detective IIs and IIIs. Dalton was a Detective II.

"You said a dead body," she questioned. "First, is it a homicide? And second, how many?"

"Security guard responding to an alarm found a man inside the house and apparently shot him. Only one DB."

Shit, Dalton thought, standing up and stretching.

"All right, Rivers," she sighed, closing her eyes. "Give me the address. I'll be there as soon as I can."

~~~

The house was typical LA Spanish influence – white stucco, red tile roof, two stories, fountain out front in a bricked courtyard and a three-car detached garage. It'd been built back when Hollywood was still fun and had survived the big shakes, including the 1994 Northridge quake which had sent a couple of neighboring homes sliding down the mountain.

A handsome wrought-iron gate affixed to the stuccoed wall surrounding the property opened onto Mulholland Drive. A patrol car now guarded the entrance, its roof lights flashing in a moderately slow tempo. Several other parked cars, some marked LAPD, stretched along the road. The cop at the gate recognized Dalton's Porsche Boxster when she drove up and waved her through.

Detective Jason Rivers stood at the doorway talking with a man in a dark suit. Parked in the courtyard was the security company's car. Dalton pulled in beside it and got out.

"Detective Dalton," Rivers said. "This is Bill Newsome. He's the president of Bonner Security."

"Did he shoot the victim?" Dalton asked.

"No, he just arrived," Rivers told her. "The security guard is inside the house. He's the one involved."

"Good," Dalton said and then turning to the other man, "Mr. Newsome, I'm going to ask you to please leave the area until we have completed our investigation."

"Detective, one of our people is involved here," Newsome protested. "You can't really expect me ...."

"I'm well aware of that, sir," Dalton said, cutting him off. "And you'll have to leave. Really."

Newsome turned to go, stopped and gave her a quizzical look, then quickly walked away.

"Take me inside, Rivers," she said.

A large foyer held a staircase leading to the second floor where there were four bedrooms. Off to the right was the living room with an adjoining library. On the left of the foyer was another even larger room that opened into a formal dining room. A staircase off the kitchen led down to an English basement, its exposed wall viewing the San Fernando Valley. The body lay on the basement floor near the foot of the stairs.

"Any identification?" Dalton asked, looking down at the dead man.

"There was nothing I could see in his front pockets," Rivers answered. "I didn't want to disturb the body by moving it."

The corpse was sprawled flat on his back, arms spread-eagle, a bullet wound below his left eye and another centered in his chest. Blood splatter was on the wall behind him. A small pool of blood had formed beneath him. He appeared to be in his late thirties.

"Must've died instantly," Rivers observed. "Not that much blood. Probably because of the round he took in the heart, huh?"

Dalton ignored the speculation and stepped around the body. She then walked over to where a door opened to the outside. The window had been smashed.

"The security guard said that's where the guy entered," Rivers volunteered. "Actually, the broken window set off the alarm."

"Detectives, the SID guy is here," a uniformed officer called down the stairs.

"All right, let's go talk with the guard," Dalton said. "They can seal off the scene until the tech has finished. But I'd like to take another look before the coroner removes the body."

~~~

Wes Albright was originally from the small town of Ridgecrest in the Mojave Desert but after having been laid off from his job there had moved to LA. He'd been with

Bonner Security for seven months.

"I worked at the weapons station," he told Dalton.

"And what did you do there?"

"I was a perimeter guard at the range. China Lake is a bombing practice area for the Navy."

Dalton nodded.

"So let's go back over what happened from the time you took the alarm call," she said. "That was around three or so this morning?"

"The dispatcher got the signal at 0235," Albright began. "I was patrolling on Coldwater Canyon. We have a number of clients there. He radioed me to check out the Hodges' house since I was closest to it."

"And you drove here immediately?" Dalton asked.

"No, I finished my rounds on Coldwater first, then I came here. Probably took maybe fifteen minutes. No longer."

Dalton and Rivers were questioning Albright in the library. He'd been taken there when Rivers had arrived on the scene. The sun was now well up and the din from the morning commute on the 101 Freeway below was beginning to rise as well.

"You answered the call alone?" Dalton asked. "No backup? Is that normal?"

"Like I said, I was the closest car to the scene. Figured I'd better not wait."

"Yet you took the time to finish your rounds. From all the way over in Coldwater Canyon, too."

Albright didn't respond.

"What about the LAPD?" Dalton continued. "Aren't they notified when a break-in's reported?"

"It's an option from what I understand," Albright explained. "Normally, the guard assigned to the area assesses the situation and decides whether or not he needs backup."

Albright seemed like a wiseguy to Dalton. She was beginning not to like him.

"So why didn't you call the police?" she asked. "I mean, an alarm had been received. You responded. Found a broken window. Didn't that tell you something?"

Albright shrugged.

"So you arrived here," Dalton said. "What next?"

"I stopped at the gate. It wasn't locked so I drove in and parked. Called the company to say that I was at the location."

"Did you request backup then?" Rivers broke in. He'd been quietly taking notes until then. Dalton shot him a look but decided that it was a reasonable enough question and, more importantly, didn't break her rhythm.

"I didn't see anything unusual so again I figured I didn't need to call," Albright said confidently.

"When *did* you see something unusual?" Dalton asked patiently.

"When I saw the broken window around back and the door was open."

Rivers rolled his eyes.

"Go on," she said.

"Well, I was suspicious so I took out my weapon and entered. It was dark inside but I thought I saw movement. Heard something. I shined my flashlight and there he was holding a gun."

"Did you identify yourself?" Dalton asked. "You know, shout something? Like security guard, hands up or whatever?"

"I don't remember. All I could see was the gun. I don't even remember firing but I guess I did, huh?"

Dalton sat quietly for a moment. Albright shifted around nervously, fidgeted with his coat sleeve.

"It wasn't a gun, Mr. Albright," she said at last. "It was a flashlight."

Albright's face blanched and he did a quick little tic-shake of his head.

"I ... it wasn't on," he stammered. "The damn thing wasn't on!"

Dalton stood.

"Mr. Albright, you're free to leave," she said. "I'd like you to come by the station in Van Nuys tomorrow morning at, say, nine o'clock. We'll go over some more questions and then I'll have you sign a statement."

Albright started to speak but instead tightened his mouth, got to his feet, and left the room.

"There were a lot of casings on the floor," Rivers said after he'd gone. "He must've emptied his gun on the poor bastard."

"What are those things?" Dalton asked, seemingly ignoring Rivers' comment and pointing to something across the room.

"What?"

"Why, they're animal skeletons, aren't they?" Dalton said incredulously, walking over to them.

Several small skeletons fully assembled and mounted on stands were placed on a side table. She bent down to examine one.

"Is that a cat?"

A uniformed officer came into the room, a strange expression on his face.

"Detectives, there's a room over the garage you ought to see."

CHAPTER 3

The garage matched the main house – white stucco with red terra-cotta tiles on the roof. Three of the doors stood open. Two bays were empty and a covered vehicle occupied the other. Outside, a set of stairs ran up behind the building to the entrance of a second-floor room.

"Looks like our intruder might've broken in here, too," a uniformed officer said.

Dalton and Rivers entered the room. Glass shards littered the floor.

"Holy crap!" Rivers exclaimed. "What the hell is this?"

The entire room was hung with heavy black draperies. An inverted cross stood at the far end and, in front of it, a gravestone served as an altar of sorts with black candles set on either side. A circled pentagram had been painted on the floor. There were no other furnishings.

"Get the photographer up here," Dalton told the officer.

~~~

It had been a long morning for Dalton and she was hoping to finish up before lunch. Earlier, officers had found a car parked in a pull-off area on Mulholland not far from the house. Registration showed it belonged to James Sterling who lived in Marina del Rey. According to ID found on the body, it was the same James Sterling that'd been tagged, bagged and delivered to the morgue. The car was towed to the Van Nuys department impound yard.

Dalton was walking wearily toward the gate when she saw a car had pulled in at the entrance and the occupants were talking with the uniformed officer stationed there. As she neared, a man on the passenger side leaned out of the window and called to her.

"Laura, it's Jack!"

~~~

"How's your salad?"

"Fine. How's your burger?"

"Not bad. Want some fries?"

Dalton and Jack Hunter were having a late lunch at a small restaurant in Studio City. They'd agreed to meet there after running into each other at the house. Mike Eaton had driven Jack back to his office to pick up his car, a red Jeep.

"Fries are full of trans fats," she said. "You shouldn't eat them."

"Yeah, but they taste so good," Jack smiled. "So what's the deal on this security guard?"

"Really can't talk about that, Jack. Right now it's an open investigation."

"Okay, when do you think I can get in the garage? I'd really like to see that car."

"Don't you think you're being a little callus?" she asked. "Person was just killed there."

"I know and I'm not being cavalier. Have to make another appointment with the estate executor and everything, that's all."

Dalton arched her eyebrows. Theirs was an odd relationship. They'd first met in Miami when she had come there to arrest him on suspicion of murder. Jack was later proven to be innocent. But their paths continued to cross in Los Angeles and even once in Key West where it had then followed a dangerous course. She'd eventually accepted him as someone of continuing mishaps which for some unknown reason, contributed to his charm. And also as someone for whom she'd developed a certain fondness. Within limits.

"I'm interviewing the security guard tomorrow morning," she said. "Depending on how that goes, I'll let you know about the garage, okay?"

Jack patted her hand.

"Thanks," he said.

~~~

That evening the local television stations reported on the shooting. The identities of Albright and James Sterling had been leaked. Footage showed the Mulholland house. A filler item included the accidental death of Martin Hodges, complete with photos of the wrecked Porsche, and a quick bio of his father, David. There was no mention of the mysterious room above the garage.

Herb Thacker, a freelance set designer who lived in Topanga Canyon, flicked off the television set and grabbed his phone.

"Did you catch the news?" he said anxiously as soon as his party picked up.

~~~

Detective Jason Rivers had earlier parked his motorcycle in the garage on the UCLA campus in Westwood and gone to the language department building for his Spanish class. This was his second year in studying the language. He'd discovered the advantage of being bilingual during his time on patrol. UCLA's night school fit his schedule and he liked his instructor.

But unfortunately tonight there'd been no class. A message scrawled on the chalkboard stated it had been cancelled. No reason given.

Disappointed, Rivers had been about to leave when he thought of the library. The bizarre room over the garage had been on his mind all afternoon. He'd taken pictures of the decor with his smartphone. Maybe the library would offer some insight.

CHAPTER 4

A thick marine layer hovered above the coast, promising to leave it shivering in gloomy fog all day, while just over the mountains LA was taking for granted another perfectly clear Southern California morning. It was that time of the year.

Jack drove along the Pacific Coast Highway to San Vicente Boulevard and turned towards Beverly Hills. He ran out of the fog just before the twin towers at Century City where Mike Eaton had his office.

"You want a cup of coffee?" Mike asked as Jack settled into a chair.

Jack, wearing a pair of jeans and a light wool sweater, nodded yes.

"Cold out your way, huh?" Mike chuckled. "We're looking for a sunny eighty degrees or so today. Hotter over in the Valley, of course."

"Lucky you," Jack said. "Talk with the lawyer yet?"

"He's good to go. One small detail, though."

Jack leaned back in his chair.

"The ex-wife is making noises," Eaton explained. "Dear 'ol Maxine. Their divorce was pretty nasty. Apparently David's lawyer was a good match for hers so she couldn't completely skin her husband alive. He'd left her pretty well off anyway. The son got the house. Everybody seemed satisfied with the settlement at the time. But now the smell of money is back in the air with the son's demise."

"Wouldn't she just inherit everything now?" Jack asked.

"She might providing there was a will. But it seems young Martin didn't bother leaving one. Now it's back to the court."

"So what does that have to do with the Jag?" Jack wanted to know. "It's in the estate. Do they want to sell it or not?"

"Oh, they want to sell it. Just might get us into a bidding war before all is said and done."

Jack considered this possibility.

"Look, why don't we try to move fast. Call the damn lawyer who's the executor. Tell him we're ready to buy today. Right now. Make him a good offer."

"What about your wanting to see the car? The cops still have the house sealed off while they figure out who dunnit."

"The car's not a suspect."

~~~

"I thought we'd have more privacy in here, sir."

Dalton showed Wes Albright into an interview room at the Van Nuys station furnished with a table and three chairs. Rivers followed Dalton in and the two detectives grabbed chairs for themselves. Dalton motioned to Albright to take the one across from them.

"Thank you for coming," Dalton began. "This shouldn't take long."

"I've already told you everything I know," Albright whined.

"Just a couple more points to cover. First, did you know the deceased?"

This threw Albright. His eyes widened.

"Know him? Hell no, I'd never seen the guy before. If I'd known him, this mess wouldn't have happened. Jesus, what a question!"

Dalton smiled.

"One of those things we have to ask, sir," she said. "But let's review what we do have so far. Want to make sure I've got everything down. Why don't we start with the time you discovered the basement door open. Now, you'd received a call and had arrived at the scene. Walked around to the rear of the house. What happened next? "

Albright swallowed.

"Well, I was suspicious, you know? I took out my gun."

"But you didn't identify yourself, is that right?" Rivers popped up. "You just walked right in without saying a word even though you were suspicious enough to take out your gun. What were you thinking?"

Dalton glared at the detective and started to say something but instead kept quiet and waited for Albright to answer.

"I ... I was doing my job," he stuttered, then took the offensive. "I don't know what I was thinking. Maybe it wasn't the smartest thing to do but you weren't in my place, were you, detective?"

"Move on to what transpired next, Mr. Albright," Dalton said firmly, flashing her eyes at Rivers.

"It was dark as hell, so I turned on my flashlight and swung the beam around the room. The guy was standing practically in front of me holding a gun. Well, I thought it was a gun. Didn't know it was just a damn flashlight. Fuck!"

Albright's voice wavered at this last and he put his hands to his face.

"I think we've finished for now, Mr. Albright," Dalton said. "We may call you back in as we continue with the investigation."

"Why?" Albright said, alarmed. "It was an accident. I'm sorry the guy's dead but I thought he had a gun!"

"A person's death is a serious matter to the Los Angeles Police Department, sir. We have to consider every possibility until proven otherwise. That's why we investigate."

"Do I need a lawyer?"

"Not at this time."

Albright let out a breath and shook his head.

"Just out of curiosity," Dalton said, "what kind of training does your company provide?"

"Bonner only hires experienced people," Albright answered, a little more in control. "But since you asked, I took the forty-hour training program and have a permit to carry the gun."

"I see. Detective Rivers will type up your statement, then take you to the front desk after you've signed it."

Dalton was at her desk when Rivers returned.

"Let's take a walk," she said, getting up.

"Great," he said eagerly. "I found out some things at the library last night I want to go over with you."

They went out to the parking lot, Dalton not speaking a word until they'd gotten there.

"Jason, you are obviously a smart person," she said. "So, what is it then? Naiveté? Lack of manners? Raised by wolves?"

In fact, Jason Rivers was very smart. He'd graduated from college in three years. Straight A's. Spent half a year trying to get a job. Not much demand for English literature majors though. Considered going into the Army. Then joined the LAPD.

"What?" he asked innocently.

"I'm talking about your interrupting me when I'm interviewing someone," Dalton told him. "Breaking the rhythm. Asking antagonizing questions. Editorializing. Do you realize the importance of all this?"

"I'm not sure I understand," he said in a slightly hurt tone.

"Jason, from now on we will discuss what's going to be said and by whom before we go into the interview room. I will be in charge of the interview and will ask the questions unless we have decided otherwise. Bad-cop good-cop routines? Again, we talk between ourselves first. I suppose I should have gone over this earlier. Are we clear?"

"Yes."

"Good. One more thing. Anyone who comes in to be interviewed is a human being no matter what he or she is suspected of doing and deserves to be treated with respect. You'll find that you get a lot more cooperation from that person when you do that."

"Thank you, detective."

Dalton looked him in the eye for a moment longer.

"Now, what was you wanted to tell me about?"

Rivers brightened.

"That weird room above the garage? I think it might've been used by a devil cult."

Dalton's mouth dropped open slightly.

"Why ever would you think that?" she asked amused.

"I took a couple of pics on my phone. Checked them out at the UCLA library last night. That symbol on the floor, black candles, all that drapery, the altar. Could've held black masses there."

"Well, that is certainly a possibility," Dalton said. "I'll mention it when I turn in my report."

Detectives in the Los Angeles Police Department are ranked I, II and III in order of investigation assignment and command. A detective one is a new arrival and works under a detective two. Both would report to the detective three in charge of their assigned crime table – homicide, robbery, theft, etc. A detective two spends most of his time in the field and, consequently, has the more challenging job. Often an officer will remain at that rank by choice for his or her entire career because of that single but important reason. The detective three's position is more managerial and can lead to moving up in the department.

Detective III Thomas Bradshaw, the head of homicide at Van Nuys, didn't want that, though. After twenty-five years with the LAPD, he'd decided long ago against becoming one of the brass and would just finish his thirty in detectives. He enjoyed his job and was good at it. He was also a hands-on cop. The top detective rank was an offer he couldn't refuse.

"So what do you want to do, Laura?" Bradshaw asked, shuffling her written report in his hands. "Think this asshole deserves a little winding up?"

"I could bring him back in for another round of questioning but I don't believe there was a crime involved. Still, I'll take the paperwork to the District Attorney. See how he feels."

"Well, you do good reports, Laura. I'm sure the DA will go along."

"Poor judgment, that's what it was. Albright was scared shitless. Panicked. If we could charge him with lack of training and general stupidity, it'd be a slam-dunk case. Wouldn't mind seeing the security company get some heat over this."

"Maybe the *Los Angeles Times* can run an expose'," Bradshaw laughed.

"Good idea. Probably should hold on to the Mulholland house until I hear back from the DA, what do you think?"

"Is there any reason not to?"

"There's a car in the garage somebody was asking about. Wants to know if he can take it."

Bradshaw shrugged.

"Just the car? Shouldn't be a problem. The shooting happened in the house. Nothing to do with the garage."

"Well, Detective Rivers might not agree," Dalton laughed. "He's concerned about some devil worshipers."

"Some who?"

"Room above the garage. It's there in the report. Looked like it might've had something to do with a cult the way the inside was done up. Spooky. Even had a real gravestone. Suppose you can get those on line."

Bradshaw leaned back in his chair and thought that over.

"Actually, the house itself would give you the creeps," Dalton continued with a little shudder. "There were all these animal skeletons sitting around. Real things. Somebody there must've had an oddball sense of decorating. I had the photographer take a couple of shots of them. You see them?"

""Yeah, interesting," Bradshaw said, arching his eyebrows. "You're right about the house being weird but I don't think the animal skeletons have anything to do with the present case. Years ago – I think it was after I came in to detectives – there was a purported rape that took place there."

"Purported?"

"Yeah, the victim decided afterwards that it'd never happened."

"My God!"

"Show business party that got out of hand," Bradshaw explained. "But everyone's innocent. Just ask them. Know what I mean?"

"Not really," Dalton said, "but I can imagine. Go ahead."

"Patrol found this woman wandering around on Mulholland in the early a.m.'s not wearing a stitch of clothes. Incoherent. Terrified. Bad shape. Took her to the ER. Examination indicated rough sex. When she was able to talk the next day, she denied anything had happened. Said she was just at a party and had had too much to drink. Didn't remember a thing."

"Did you investigate?" Dalton asked incredulously.

"Of course we did," Bradshaw told her, taken aback. "No witnesses. Nothing came of it."

"Jesus," Dalton said. "The poor woman. Those rotten bastards got away with it."

'Yeah," Bradshaw agreed. ""How is Rivers coming along?"

"He's learning."

CHAPTER 5

The attraction of a Jaguar E-type is pure sex. No other car even comes close to its turn-on. Jack couldn't take his eyes off the sleek, beautiful shape. Even more incredible was the fact that this racy baby was now his.

"What do you think?" Mike Eaton grinned.

"When's the flatbed coming?" Jack answered.

"The parts are in those boxes next to the wall," Ed Stone interrupted. He was the executor of the estate.

"Should be another thirty minutes," Mike told Jack. "That okay with you, Ed? Stick around until the tow truck gets here?"

"Sure. You want to load the boxes in your car or let the truck driver take them?"

The deal had included a number of original factory parts which would be nearly impossible to find available today. Getting the spare parts helped to soften the heavy blow they'd been dealt by the staggering price they had settled on. Jack wasn't one to profligate but this *was* an XKE.

"Wait for the truck," Jack decided. "Better to keep the parts with the car."

Once the sale had been completed, Ed Stone had called Van Nuys LAPD to find out when they could remove the car. To everyone's relief the garage wasn't part of the investigation.

"There's a storage facility I use," Mike said. "Hanger out at Burbank Airport. Good security. Want to take everything there?"

"Thanks, Mike," Jack grinned, "but right now I'd rather have it in my garage. First thing I'm going to do is sit in it and have a drink."

~~~

The fucking tow truck wouldn't let him pass. He'd been stuck behind it all the way up Laurel Canyon and now it'd turned onto Mulholland the same way he was going. Just his luck! Probably some idiot's Rolls Royce had a dead battery. There was nothing he could do but poke along behind it.

Herb Thacker had been in Hollywood working on a set at a soundstage. It'd been a three-day build for a television commercial. Filming was scheduled to start tomorrow and the pouty little shit of a director was still making changes to the set. The irritating truck slowed to a crawl, then stopped completely. Right in the middle of the goddamn road! He laid on the horn. The truck driver glared back at him in the rearview mirror and crept ahead to the next driveway, stopped again and then drove in. Herb couldn't believe it had come to this very house.

~~~

"About time you got here," Mike Eaton said good-naturedly.

"Wasn't sure of the address, sir," the driver explained. "That the car?"

The Jag had been rolled out of the garage and into the courtyard. The hood was raised and the trunk lid open. Jack had removed a black metal case from inside the trunk and was now examining it.

"Locked," he muttered. "You know where the key is to this thing, Ed?"

"Probably in one of those other boxes," the lawyer told him. "Along with the owner's manual and tool kit."

"Wonder what's inside?"

"Probably a special tool for the car, Jack," Eaton guessed. "You know, came from the factory in England."

"Think so?" Jack questioned. "What about that, Ed? Goes with the car?"

"Painted black, isn't it?"

Jack nodded, placed the case back into the trunk and shut the lid.

Thacker, who'd been watching from his car at the top of the driveway, quietly drove off.

At 4 a.m. the next morning, the alarm rang in the Sherman Oaks fire station.

~~~

"This is crazy," Dalton said to the fireman.

She was at the Hodges house on Mulholland. The garage had burned during the night. A neighbor had reported the fire after being awakened by the sound of a car speeding away. The blaze had been quickly extinguished once the fireman had arrived. Most of the damage was confined to the upper room.

LAPD had also responded. Dalton was told about the blaze when she'd come to the station and had gone directly there. The building was still smoldering and a few of the firemen were working to completely quench any remaining embers. This was heavy fire season in Southern California.

"I don't know what they kept in here," the fireman said. "Apparently, the walls were covered by heavy fabric. Like draperies. You can see a little of the material still left hanging on the curtain rods. Certainly wasn't fireproof."

The entire room was gutted.

"Do you have any idea about how the fire started?" Dalton asked.

"There's a lot of what appears to be wax by that table," he said. "Pooled up on the floor. Looks like it might've been from candles. My guess would be that's where it started. Whether by accident or something else is another question. The arson investigator will determine that."

Dalton looked around at the blackened room. It smelled of evil.

"This house is cursed," she muttered.

She walked away from the garage and around to the rear of the main house where she discovered a path leading down to a small potting shed with an adjoining glass hothouse. She pushed open the door. A horrible odor greeted her.

~~~

The detectives room at the police station was a large area furnished with groupings of desks referred to as *tables*. Each table was composed of four desks and assigned to investigate certain crime categories. Robbery, Burglary, Auto Theft. Assault With A Deadly Weapon, Homicide. A Detective III sat at the head of the table with a couple of I's and II's on either side.

"Here's the thing," Dalton said, sitting at her desk next to Tom Bradshaw. "The fire at the Hodges place was in that weird room above the garage."

"The devil chapel, right?"

"You're talking about the markings on the floor. Yeah, the inverted pentagram's supposed to help conjure up spirits, according to our expert, Jason."

"Does it look like arson?" Bradshaw asked.

"Maybe or it could've been accidental. The room had draperies covering all the walls. A lot of candles placed around. Firemen believe the candles may have set the fabric on fire."

"So what's your take?" Bradshaw asked. "Security guy shoots a prowler, now this fire."

"I believe James Sterling was familiar with the location. And he wasn't just a random prowler, either. The first place he broke into was that room above the garage, not the main house where you'd expect to find expensive items. Apparently the garage wasn't connected to the alarm system. Otherwise the security company would've been notified earlier and might've gotten there sooner. But whatever it was he'd wanted wasn't there. So he hit the house and we know what happened next."

"Why now?" Bradshaw asked. "The owner's been dead for two months."

"Maybe he was waiting for the caretaker to leave," Dalton answered. "Or it could have something to do with the estate being settled."

"Do you have a line on the caretaker? Might like to talk with him or her."

"We're working on it."

"Back to the garage being his first choice," Bradshaw said. "A little odd don't you think?"

"Maybe and maybe not. I thought about Jason's findings at the library. If the garage was some kind of meeting place for the occult, then others are involved. And more importantly, what the hell goes on in those meetings?"

"Let's ask Rivers," Bradshaw said. "Where is he, by the way?"

"He's doing a follow-up on that ADW involving the contractor," she told him. "You remember, the guy who hit a worker over the head with a caulking gun? Gave him eight stitches."

"Right, used a caulking gun," Bradshaw chuckled, "I wonder if that qualifies for an enhancement charge."

CHAPTER 6

"It was in the damn trunk! Fucking idiot."

"So what do we do now?"

"We get it back."

Herb Thacker ended the call and slipped the phone back into his pocket. The filming at the studio had been tedious and they were behind schedule at the end of the day. No way would they wrap tomorrow. Not unless they went into platinum time and, with a crew as large as this one, the producer had decided it would be cheaper just to add another day to the shoot. He walked out onto the wide deck.

The house stood halfway up the mountain and provided an excellent view of the canyon cutting through to the Pacific Ocean. You couldn't live in a better place, except for the occasional time when the Santa Ana winds are blowing and some crazy puts a match to the impenetrable Manzanita shrub and turns the mountains into hell.

God, he muttered aloud and thought, if only Sterling had looked in that car. It was the obvious place for Martin to have kept the case. Well, they'd just have to find the new owner. Actually, that shouldn't be too hard, come to think of it.

Heh, did he just say *God*? Now there's a laugh for you.

~~~

The animal skeletons kept cropping up in Dalton's mind. Especially the cat's. She pictured her own cat at home. Well, hopefully it was at home. The ungrateful beast she'd taken in at her old place had worried her so much with its frequent disappearances. So like a cat! She'd brought it with her when she moved to the wonderful guesthouse on a property in Encino. Only to have the thing once more gallivanting around to heaven knows where. A worry without end.

Tom Bradshaw approached the table and interrupted her thoughts.

"I asked a friend of mine about those animal bones at the Hodges'," he said. "Showed him the photographs."

Dalton looked up in surprise.

"I was just thinking about them," she said.

"He's a veterinarian," Bradshaw continued. "I was curious myself. Anyway, he identified a couple of cats, a dog and then one was a goat, if you can believe that."

"People have weird tastes," Dalton shrugged.

"The goat was interesting," Bradshaw went on. "Dogs and cats are everywhere but you'd have to go out of your way to find a goat. That's intriguing in light of Rivers' research on the occult. Small animals, and particularly goats, are often sacrificed during a ritual."

"I must be missing something here, boss," Dalton smiled. "Sacrifices?"

"If that garage was some kind of dark chapel like Rivers believes, then you have to wonder what all went on there. I'm not so old that I don't remember the Manson Family."

The Manson Family was a drug-fueled cult founded by Charles Manson, a 32-year-old who'd spent a couple of decades in and out of jail. He'd established himself as the guru of a new spiritual community founded on various religious theologies, including Satanism. In 1969, its members murdered eight people on Charlie's orders. The actress, Sharon Tate, who was pregnant at the time, being among their victims.

"I walked around the property," Dalton said. "Area out back smells awful. Wonder if we should look into it?"

"Have to get a court order," Bradshaw mused. "No

probable cause."

"Just a thought," Dalton smiled.

"Funny thing about goats," Bradshaw said with a mischievous grim. "Got a mind of their own. Community up north hired out goats to keep down unwanted vegetation. Part of the fire defense plan, they said. About sixty of them were chomping away on a hillside when they decided the grass was greener on the other side. Knocked down an eight-foot fence to get into the backyard of someone's house. Ate everything in sight. Stripped the rose bushes, munched the hydrangeas, azaleas – you name it, they ate it. Owner ran out into the yard to chase them away and left the back door open. You can imagine what happened next."

"Did you learn that from your veterinarian friend?" Dalton asked suspiciously.

"Just trying to get your goat," Bradshaw guffawed.

~~~

Winston's was a greasy spoon on Van Nuys Boulevard a couple of blocks from the police station. Its location made it a favorite lunch spot for cops.

"That was a good follow-up on the ADW," Dalton said to Rivers. "The DA's going to bust that jerk's balls."

She and Rivers were having lunch, at her invitation.

"Thanks," Rivers beamed. "Oh, I've got some more info from the library."

Dalton smiled.

"There are three types of Satanism," he told her. "Type one is heavy-duty devil worshipers. Two and three are more unorganized. All of them perform sacrifices. Usually sacrificial bodies won't be found. They're moved so the soul can come back later and reclaim them. Types two and three sometimes leave the body, however. But to make it more confusing, Type one will also occasionally leave a burned body at the site."

"Back up a moment," Dalton said, holding up her hand. "Are you talking about animal or human bodies?"

"Both, but like I said, leaving a body behind is rare with type one. That's because the blood and other parts are used in the ceremony."

Dalton's appetite walked out the door at that point. Rivers shook some ketchup from the bottle onto his fries.

"Jason, I want you to look into Martin Hodges," she said, turning her head away as the detective forked a load of fries into his mouth. "Find out everything you can about his habits, friends, whatever. Also the same on his old man."

"David Hodges was around during the Manson killings," Rivers said, pausing to shovel in the last of his fries. "But I don't think this thing is cult-related. The Manson Family was into helter-skelter mass murder. Satanism is complex, organized, ritualistic. Charley was an egotistical nutcase who needed attention and liked to get laid a lot. Communes were popular back then. So were cults. The Manson Family became a perfect fit for him."

"Interesting analyses," Dalton said, reaching into her purse for a credit card. "One more thing. This is between you and me. For the time being anyway. So keep a tight lip. You ready to head back to the office?"

CHAPTER 7

"Jack, you interested in flipping the Jag?"

Jack had been on the deck of the Malibu house when the telephone rang. Caller ID had said it was Mike Eaton.

"Flipping?" he laughed. "You must've flipped, Mike. Hell, no. Why do you ask?"

A gentle surf washed the beach. He got up from the deck chair and stepped inside.

"I have another party interested in a Series 1" Mike said. "Suppose to drop by this afternoon. Okay, if I show them the pictures of yours? Kind of give 'em an idea of the cars out there, although that baby you got is exceptional."

The surf picked up with a rogue set of boomers. Jack slid the glass door shut to block out the noise.

"That's fine, Mike. Just be sure to tell 'em they can't have it."

"Will do, Jack. I'm going to email you a couple of names of mechanics who're really good with Jaguars. One's down in Orange County. Then there's another guy up near Santa Barbara."

"I was thinking about Eric Nystrom in Carmel. You know anything about him?"

"Nystrom? Yeah, he's done a couple of cars for the Monterey show."

"I haven't decided yet. Shoot me those other guys' names. Say, remember that damn black box? Couldn't find the key for it? Whatshisname said it was in with the other stuff. Well, it's not."

"Shit. I called Ed Stone about that key earlier. He said he'd check with Maxine but I wouldn't put much hope in that. She's pissed off at him for selling the car. Can you break the lock?"

"Rather not have to. The box is kind of nice."

"Take it to a locksmith."

~~~

Dalton turned off Ventura Boulevard onto Topanga Canyon. Jack had invited her to dinner and she was on her way to meet him. There was a great place just past Trancas Beach that'd been there forever and so far hadn't been ruined by the moneyed crowd.

By happenstance, Mike Eaton was three cars behind her and had made the same turn onto the boulevard himself. Neither one was aware of the other. Mike's client for the Jag had called earlier claiming he couldn't make the afternoon appointment with him at Century City and wondering if he'd mind coming to his place in Topanga. He was on his way there now. After all, a hot client ready to buy a bill-and-a-half car didn't waltz in every day.

Traffic in front of him turned off and he noticed the Boxster up ahead. The Porsche looked familiar but then why wouldn't it? The marque's practically an entitlement in LA. His professional side got the better of him and he did a mental appraisal on the car. Earlier year beginning to show its age. Low-book value at best.

The road opened up and the Porsche sped away, a lithe spirit at one with the curvy canyon road.

At Fernwood, Mike Eaton took a sharp left turn taking him up the mountain. A few minutes later he'd arrived at the address and pulled into the drive, parking behind another vehicle, a large pickup . The house was set back on a secluded lot.

"Mike Eaton, I presume," Herb Thacker greeted, leisurely walking up to Mike's Honda Accord and extending his hand. "I'm Aleister Crowley. Hope it wasn't a problem for you to come."

Herb had thought it'd be a joke to give the name of long-dead Satanist Aleister Crowley when he'd inquired about the car.

"Not at all, Mr. Crowley," Mike smiled. "Am I blocking someone in?"

"Nothing to worry about," Thacker said, clapping him on the shoulder. "Friend of mine. He's interested in the Jag, too."

Well, well, Mike thought, could there be a little bidding war developing?

"I've brought a few pictures of some possible cars for you to consider," he said. "They're all comparable to the one you called about, Mr. Crowley."

"Hey, it's Al, okay? I'm sure they're lovely. Still, I'd really like to see that XKE you recently found. Think that would be possible? We could go take a look."

"With all respect, Al, we're strict about client confidentiality. I did pass on your interest in the car to the new owner but he's solid. It's really not for sale."

"Maybe if I could talk with him, the owner? Price really isn't a problem. If you'd give me his name and address, then I'll get in touch with him. Leave you out of it altogether. Oh, and don't worry. I'll pay your commission."

"I'm sorry. I can't divulge that information."

Herb smiled.

"I understand," he said. "Let's go inside and see what you have. Maybe you'll change your mind about showing the other car."

~~~

Dalton had met Jack at his house and they'd driven in his Jeep up the PCH to Latigo Canyon where the restaurant was located.

"How do you like being back in the seventies?" Jack grinned, once they'd been seated.

"I'm expecting to be beamed up any minute now," Dalton said.

The waiter arrived with menus. He looked like a good

fit for the seventies himself. Ponytail, laid back attitude with a slightly stoned demeanor.

"The halibut's fresh," he stated. "You'll love it."

They both ordered it, brushed with olive oil and broiled. Salad on the side. The waiter, his name was Wavy Gravy, smiled and left.

"Well, I have to say that's some car you bought, Jack."

"Someone already wants to buy it from me," he laughed. "Mike Eaton called and said he had a guy who was interested."

"Are you going to sell it?"

"Not a chance. Wait until you ride in that thing."

"Hope it's better than your Jeep."

"What, old red isn't good enough for you?" Jack laughed.

The Jeep was an early C5 model, one favored by purists, a little touchy in handling but definitely cool. The suspension had been tricked out in Jack's C5, however, lowered and given a wider stance. It cornered like it was on rails. And a few goodies done to the engine just for fun. With the mechanical fixes done, he'd had it painted fire engine red.

"I forgot to ask," Wavy said, returning to the table. "Would you like anything to drink? We have an excellent wine list."

They declined, saying water would be fine.

"Maybe a glass or two when we get back to the house?" Jack suggested. "You can stay over in the guest bedroom."

"Can't do, Jack. I want to be at roll call tomorrow morning."

"I get up with the pelicans."

She smiled.

"Tempting but the answer is still no. But be sure to thank your bird friends for me."

"You know how to break a guy's heart. Look, I want to

ask you something that just came to mind. About that black metal case I showed you. Locksmith can't open it. So I was wondering if there's anyone where you work who's good at picking locks? I mean, I've seen that sort of thing on television."

Dalton laughed.

"Columbo returns?" she said. "I'm not surprised. Actually, we do have an in-house yegg. That's a safecracker, in case Colombo didn't tell you. Bring the thing in tomorrow around ten."

Wavy arrived with their orders. He was right about the halibut.

~~~

Jack awoke to the sound of movement outside the house. He sat up and looked at the bedside clock. 3:30 a.m. Then a car door slammed shut. Getting out of bed he went to the window in time to see a car drive off. It was a foreign make. For some odd reason, he sensed a strange vibe. He couldn't get back to sleep.

~~~

The pelicans hadn't been awakened in the middle of the night and no doubt were feeling a little more bright-eyed than Jack the next morning. Nevertheless, he was at Van Nuys LAPD with black box in hand promptly at ten o'clock. The desk officer called Detectives.

"Jack, this is Vic Young," Dalton said, coming through the door with a man in tow wearing a Hawaiian shirt and chino pants. "Detective Young works theft and knows more about how to open a lock than Houdini."

"What've we got here, Jack?" Young said, eyeing the black box.

"Apparently something made with Fort Knox in mind," Jack said. "This thing was in the trunk of a car I just bought. Suppose to have a key somewhere but I can't find it. So I took it to a locksmith but he couldn't open it.

Said I had to find the place that sold the lock and get them to make a key. Nobody else could do it."

Jack handed the box to the detective.

"Well, he was right," Young said, examining the lock. "This is a high-security lock. Got a billion keying combinations. Even the keys have a special side-cut. Thing's strong as a tank. Take a look here."

He pointed at the face or the lock.

"That cylinder's hardened steel. Almost impossible to drill through."

Jack's face fell.

"So you're saying it can't be opened without a key?"

Young ran his hand over the box's surface.

"Somebody went to a lot of trouble installing that lock. Nice work. I recognize the type of case. It's for carrying cameras and lenses. You can buy ones similar to it at a photography store. But this one is professional quality. Probably from a supply house. Be a shame to ruin it."

Jack shrugged.

"I don't think it belongs with the car," he said. "Guy thought it might've come from the Jaguar factory but you're right, it *is* a camera case. I've seen them before when I used to work in the ad agency business."

"Let's step outside to my office," the detective gestured.

The three of them walked out to the station's parking lot.

"Locks are a hobby of mine," he commented on the way. "Comes in handy occasionally in my line of work."

They arrived at Young's car and he popped open the trunk and took out a portable electric drill.

"Hold this for a minute, Jack. I've got a circle saw somewhere in here."

After rummaging through a toolbox he'd found what he was looking for and attached it to the drill.

"I'm just going to cut the lock out of the camera case."

In short order the saw had chewed through the metal around the lock. Jack and Laura crowded around as Young opened the top.

"My God!" she gasped.

A human skull grinned up at her.

~~~

"The medical examiner is sending someone," Tom Bradshaw reported, returning from the lieutenant's office.

They'd gathered at the Homicide Table. The group included Dalton, Rivers and Young.

"Man, I don't know which was worse," Young said. "Seeing that damn skull or the hands."

The skull had been nestled in a cutout section of foam rubber. On either side of it was a human hand placed palms up, its bones wired together and articulated.

"Maybe it's a piece for Dia de los Muretes," Rivers joked.

"Wonder if it's all the same person," Dalton grimaced, paying no mind to his humor about the Day of the Dead.

"Well, the ME can determine that," Bradshaw told her. "The remains don't appear to be all that old, I mean they aren't ancient. So we can probably get some DNA. Check dental charts with missing persons. Also, they'll be looking for prints on the skull and inside the box. Your boyfriend holding up okay, Laura?"

"He's not exactly my boyfriend, Tom," she told him testily. "But yes, he's all right. He's probably home by now. I'll call to check after we're done here."

~~~

Jack had indeed returned to the Malibu house. He'd also phoned the security company as soon as he had walked in. A man was due that afternoon to check on the house's system and see if it could be improved in any way.

The commotion in the driveway last night had set off

an alarm in Jack's head, a little red warning light that he wasn't about to ignore. It had saved him more than once while down range in Iraq.

He probably should've mentioned the incident to Laura. But then, what was it anyway? Most likely some jerk pulling over to puke after the last bar closed. Still.

He'd earlier given Mike Eaton a call only to have it go to message. Now he tried again. Same deal. That was too bad because he'd wanted to talk with him about the Jag. Let him know that he was going with Eric Nystrom for the restoration work. The doorbell rang.

"Mr. Hunter? I'm Dan Dudley with Courtney Security."

Jack invited him in.

"I've brought a schematic of your present plan," Dudley said. "Took awhile to find it in our records."

"So what do you think?" Jack asked. "Keep out the bad guys?"

"State of the art stuff," Dudley said. "Twenty-five years ago maybe. Tell you the truth, sir, I could get through this system in a lazy minute. High school kid in probably half the time."

"That good a system, huh?"

"I would suggest a major upgrade if you're really serious. Include some strategic camera locations both inside and outside. You could have a split-screen monitor in the master bedroom, another downstairs, perhaps in the kitchen, and we would have a feed to our office which would be activated should there be an incursion. And then would automatically notify the local police."

"Sounds good," Jack nodded. "Let's get started."

CHAPTER 8

The LA County Sheriffs Department cruiser bounced along the uneven dirt road leading to the dry lake near Lancaster. Ten or twenty thousand years ago, the sun would have reflected off a shallow body of water here but today the surface was hard-packed clay and crisscrossed with cracks.

The road flattened out onto the broad lakebed itself and the car sped up. Its destination a dot floating above a shimmering mirage.

Closer now, the deputy could see an old Ford Bronco parked next to another vehicle. Two people stood by the Ford.

"Are you the folks that called?" Deputy Charles Brinkley asked, getting out of his cruiser and approaching the couple, a man and a young boy.

"Yes, sir," the man said. "My name's Wade Davis."

The deputy glanced over at the burned car.

"You don't want to look in there for long," Wade warned. "We sometimes come here to hunt for scrap metal and any lumber that might be good. People filming television commercials leave stuff others can use. Anyway, we saw the car and drove out to it."

"What's your name, son?" Brinkley asked the boy.

"Kenny, sir."

"Well, you stay here with your dad, Kenny."

The deputy walked over to the car, not more than a charred hulk of metal. The tires had burned down to the rims, its windows were blackened and very little was left inside other than the remains of a human seated behind the steering wheel.

~~~

"If the locking area of that case had been backed with steel, we'd been screwed and tattooed," Vic Young allowed. "I couldn't have cut through it with my tools."

He was holding court with Dalton and Rivers around the coffee machine.

"Had to have taken it to a machine shop then and got them to drill out the lock with a diamond-tip bit," he added.

"I like that idea," Dalton said. "Let someone else be the first to see what was inside."

"Skull's the first thing people look at when they see a skeleton," Rivers chimed in. "Irresistible."

Dalton gave him a not-so-nice look of her own.

"True fact," he went on obliviously. "Out of the whole human skeleton, the skull's the big deal. Draws you in. Eye sockets do the trick. Here's another one. Did you know that archeologists can spot a piece of the skull hidden in a pile of rocks? Stands out. It's who we are when we were alive."

"That's sick," Dalton told him.

"Think so? What did Hamlet say in the graveyard when he held up that head bone? 'Alas, poor Yorick! I knew him well, Horatio ...' See?"

"Guess you didn't sleep through all of your classes," Dalton smirked.

"Actually, I did," Rivers admitted with a grin. "But English lit was a favorite."

"What about those hands?" Young said quietly. "Creepy, man."

"Intimacy there," Rivers said professorially. "Knowledge of the spirit they belonged to, that's what the hands give. Especially if the bones haven't been bleached."

"Are you serious?" Dalton asked. "Someone would actually play hands with those things?"

"I'm into this bones business," Rivers laughed. "Really,

the library's a great place for information. People seem to have forgotten that. But since then I've gone online. You'd be amazed at what you can find there about cults and rituals. Check it out."

"Back to the camera case for a minute," Young said. "The guy who worked on it knew what he was doing. Probably owned a shop or at least had some good equipment. Knew about locks, too."

Dalton perked her ears.

"Didn't you say something about having to take the lock to where it was bought to have a key made for it?"

"Yeah, it has a serial number on it. The manufacturer can tell you who the distributor was."

All three detectives looked at one another.

~~~

The body discovered in the burned-out car had been taken to the LA County Morgue where it was placed on a gurney, registered and rolled into a room already crowded to capacity with the dead, each awaiting its turn on the autopsy table.

Sheriffs Detective Emilio Zaragoza from the Homicide Bureau had been assigned to the case.

Though the license plates had been removed, the VIN number showed that the car had last belonged to Michael Eaton. Zaragoza ran Eaton's name with the DMV and got back a drivers license showing the picture of a white male who weighed 165 pounds and had brown eyes and blonde hair. The burnt thing taken from the car had been unidentifiable. He took note of the address and looked up its telephone number in the backward phone directory. The reference book was a relic from the past that still had use in the digital age. There was a listing with an 818 area code. He called and got voice mail.

Leaving a message, he next checked the stolen vehicle list against the plate number he'd also gotten from DMV.

Not there, but maybe it hadn't been reported.

One more call.

"Los Angeles Police Department, Van Nuys Division," the desk officer answered.

"This is Detective Emilio Zaragoza with the LA Sheriffs. One of our deputies found a DB in a burned car in the desert near Lancaster. Car's registered to a Mike Eaton. Lives in Sherman Oaks. I've called the number at the residence but nobody's home. Could one of your men check on it for us? Heck of a drive from where I am. Sure would appreciate the help."

"I'll give it to patrol. How's the weather out your way?

"Hotter'n hell."

~~~

Jack had no luck reaching Mike on his cell. He phoned the Century City office.

"Eaton Classic Cars," a woman answered.

"Hi Brenda, this is Jack Hunter. Mike in?"

"Hello, Mr. Hunter. Mike hasn't been in all day. Did you try him at home?"

Brenda Carson was a 24-year-old aspiring actress who'd moved to LA from Columbus, Ohio, where she she'd spent a few seasons with a repertory company. So far her agent had gotten her a couple of TV commercials which, as she was quick to say, buys the groceries.

"Yeah, I called there and then his cell and now you. Look, when he does come in, have him ring me, okay?"

"Will do, Mr. Hunter. Hey, I've got a commercial tonight on the Channel 7 news. Olsen Ford at six fifteen. It's local but what the heck, it buys the groceries."

"I'll be sure to watch, Brenda. Don't forget to ask Mike to call."

Jack hung up and went out on his deck. Couple thousand miles to the west Hawaii was still looking at a few more hours of sunshine. Malibu would soon be turning on the lights. Now'd be a nice time to go for a walk. Watch the stars come to life. Be great except you'd be flattened by traffic on California Route 1 the minute you stepped outside. Nobody walks on the Pacific Coast Highway unless he's suicidal.

For that matter, hardly anyone ever walked anywhere in LA. You wonder why they even bothered putting in sidewalks. That's one of the many things he missed about Key West. If he were there in his house on Ashe Street right now, he'd stroll down to the Bight and check out the yachts. Maybe drop by the little Tiki for a drink while the sun sinks into the Gulf of Mexico and everyone sends up a big cheer at Mallory Square. Or head up Duval Street just to take in the sights. Point being he could walk to wherever he wanted.

Just getting into the night in Key West, too. He toyed with the idea of calling Billy Bean at the restaurant. But then what? He went inside and picked up the keys to the Jeep.

The drive up Malibu Canyon to Monte Nido took on a magical quality as the day began to abandon the mountains. He pulled into the lot at a rustic restaurant hidden in a grove of California oak trees. Just as he was getting out of the Jeep, a siren from the county fire station began to wail and set the hills to song from the coyotes. The siren faded, having only run a test, and the howls quickly dwindled to a few yips and yaps before dying out completely. It was a moment not to have been missed.

Jack ordered a glass of red wine at the bar and took it outside to a seating area. The western sky blazed with the last of the sun. And the air held its warmth for a little longer before relinquishing it to the cool evening. A scent of sagebrush. Ah, California, he thought.

It was odd about Mike. Not returning a call wasn't like him. The old guy was usually on top of things. Maybe he'd fallen or something? An accident. Like they say, most accidents happen at home, right? If he hadn't heard back from him by morning, he'd drive to the house and see what was going on. He took a sip of wine and leaned back in his chair.

The Jaguar came to mind. Tomorrow he would inventory all the spare parts and make a list of what he wanted done to the car. Then he'd call Eric Nystrom.

Twilight ebbed to darkness. A few stars burned dimly overhead while a marine layer began to drift in from the sea bringing a chill to the air. Jack finished his wine and left for home. The canyon was cold and he wished he'd worn a sweater. At last he swung into his drive. When he opened the front door, he felt cold, too. The deck door stood wide open.

~~~

"Your house is clear, Mr. Hunter," the deputy announced.

Jack had immediately called the LA Sheriffs when he'd discovered the open door off the deck. To their credit, two cruisers had arrived within minutes.

"Probably came in off the deck." the officer pointed out. "You can put a pin through the door and the frame which works pretty good. Or cut off a broom handle and lay it in the track."

The place hadn't been totally tossed but it was apparent that someone had been there rummaging around. Couple of closet doors left standing open, some drawers gone through. Jack went into the garage. A few of the parts boxes had been ripped open but fortunately the Jag hadn't been touched. He returned to the living room.

"Obviously someone was looking for something specific," the deputy commented. "Any respectable burglar would've grabbed those horns."

He pointed to two saxophones cradled in stands next

to a keyboard.

"Yeah, obviously," Jack said. "Whatever it is, I wish they'd just asked. Save everybody a lot of trouble."

"Can you tell if anything is missing, sir?"

"I can't say. Maybe after I straighten up. The ironic thing is that I just talked with my security company today. Having a whole new system put in. Isn't that something?"

"Were there any firearms in the house?" the deputy asked. "That would be helpful for us to know."

Jack looked at the deputy.

"No," he answered. "I've seen enough of guns. Don't keep any around."

The sheriffs left and Jack walked through the house again, taking in each room. He decided he'd wait until the morning to put things back in order. Right now he felt completely out on his feet and the bed was starting to look good.

CHAPTER 9

D alton inched along the 101 to the 134, where traffic picked up briskly until the LA Zoo then slowed once more to a crawl. She merged into the far right lane and onto the 5, passing by the Police Academy which never failed to stir a few memories. So long ago yet like yesterday. At last she came to the off-ramp that put her on the surface streets leading to the Los Angeles County morgue.

For once she was happy to be inside the frigid building. High nineties were forecast for downtown LA by noon. Van Nuys was already an oven. She asked at the reception desk for Dr. John Logan.

"Glad you could come, detective," Logan greeted, coming out into the room. "Let's go back to where we can talk."

Dalton followed the medical examiner down a hallway past the examining rooms to a small office. She couldn't help but notice the unpleasant smell. It was all too familiar from the many autopsies she'd attended.

"Grab a chair," Logan offered, sitting himself behind a desk. "I've sent my report on the skull and hands to your department, but I wanted to further discuss the findings with you."

He reached into a folder and removed some photographs.

"This one shows the base of the skull. You can see the bone is chipped at the C1 vertebrae location. That tells us it wasn't a surgical decapitation but rather crudely done."

He picked up another photo.

"This a picture of the wrists on the hands. Same deal there. Chopped off."

Dalton's expression had grown grim.

"Can you tell if it's the same person?" she asked. "I mean, the skull and the hands. Also, would the person have been alive when it was done?"

"There's no way to tell whether he was alive or not from what we have. This was a male, by the way. So we can't rule homicide in or out. We're running tests on DNA taken from the teeth and marrow left in the fingers. Should have results soon, believe it or not. Usually there's the standard up to eighteen months wait. I believe it might be a single individual. The age of the bones match. Also, we can see if there's a match in the DNA base. I've x-rayed the teeth. You can check dental records on missing persons."

Dalton shook her head.

"Who would do something like this? And why? And another thing. How did they get it so ... clean?"

Logan took a deep breath before answering.

"As far as who and why, it's possible you're looking at ritual use. Certain groups believe bones have special powers."

"The room above the garage was spooky enough," Dalton said. "There was a pentagram painted on the floor. Also a headstone apparently used for some kind of altar."

"Yes, but I have another reason for my suspicions. I discovered trace amounts of Biotex in the skull and on the hand bones. It's a washing powder with enzymes. I've already mentioned this to Detective Bradshaw. He told me about some animal skeletons at the Hodges house. I requested he send me one. And, as you have probably guessed, the same enzyme showed up."

Dalton's face paled.

"As to the cleansing of the bones" Logan continue, "there are two methods. Dermestes uses skin beetles to clean off the flesh. Maceration lets the carcass rot inside a closed container at a constant temperature. It's a pretty smelly process."

Logan pulled a face. Dalton tried not to even imagine either one. Then she remembered the hothouse at the estate and that putrid odor. She made a mental note to take a second look there.

"Would the cleaning affect the DNA?" she asked.

"Not if we get it from the teeth because in them it's protected. I'm confident they'll provide us with what we need. Incidentally, did you know that there are only three human DNA on the planet?"

"What?"

"That's true," Logan grinned. "Black, White and Asian. That basic marker will always be present."

"Amazing," Dalton commented. "Back to the cleansing business, why do people do it?"

"Most of the time, maceration is done for educational purposes," Logan explained. "Say an articulated skeleton for an anatomy class. Since this case is a forensic investigation with the possibility of a crime having been committed, we're considering other reasons."

"What about making a sketch of the face?" Dalton asked.

"I was about to get to that," Logan told her. "That can be done on a computer. What happens is the anthropological landmarks are located on the face, then careful measurements are taken for placement of ears and such. Next, soft tissue is next added by computer and the face is built up. The old way was to use a clay material for this the way a sculptor might, referencing the same landmarks, of course. It was slow and expensive but with the right person doing the work, you'd end up with a pretty good likeness. With the computer it's called geometric modeling and it can be done in 3D."

"That's really something," Dalton said. "I knew about

the clay sculpting but the computer is a new one."

"Only a few labs are using 3D computers right now. You'd still have to guess color of hair and eyes, though."

Dalton thought that over.

"How soon can we get a 3D image done?" she asked.

"I'll look into it," Logan said. "We may have enough of the skeleton – that is, the hands and skull providing they're from the same person as I said – to tell us the age, height and race, too."

~~~

Jack was just walking around to the front from the backyard of the house when the LAPD patrol car stopped at the curb. He'd driven to Sherman Oaks after phoning Mike Eaton earlier and not getting an answer.

"You live here, sir?" the officer called to him.

"No, my friend does," Jack answered.

"What's his name?"

"Mike Eaton."

"Is Mr. Eaton at home?"

"I don't know. He isn't answering the door. I'm concerned about him."

The policeman said something into his shoulder mike, then turned his attention back to Jack.

"Could I see some identification, please?" he asked.

"Sure," Jack said, taking out his billfold and removing his driver's license. "May I ask what's going on here?"

"Seems Mr. Eaton's car was found abandoned," the cop said, returning the license. "Could've been stolen."

Jack gasped.

"My God, is Mike all right?"

"We haven't been able to locate him yet."

A foreboding swept over Jack.

"You say his car was stolen. Where was it found?"

"Sheriffs district. Didn't tell us where."

"Do you usually try to track down the owner like this?"

"We're just assisting the sheriffs office."

Something didn't sound right, Jack thought.

"I've been trying to get hold of him since yesterday," he said. "Went by his office in Century City. They haven't heard from him either."

"How well do you know Mr. Eaton? Is he prone to disappearances?"

"Well, I really can't say. Mike deals in classic cars. I was in the market for one. He had been looking around."

"And did he find you a car?"

What the hell does that have to do with this, Jack wondered to himself.

"Actually, he did," Jack told him. "Not far from here, in fact. Estate up on Mulholland. Hodges. Had a shooting there, maybe you remember?"

The officer looked at his partner and then back to Jack.

"One more thing, sir. Is this Mike Eaton?"

He held a fax of Eaton's drivers license picture.

"Yeah, that's Mike."

~~~

The *Times* had run a small story on page 8 about a body being found in a car on a dry lakebed in today's edition. Los Angeles Sheriffs were investigating, it had stated.

"I bet the fuckers are investigating," Herb Thacker smirked aloud, folding up the newspaper and dropping it to the floor. He was stretched out in a lounge on the deck of his house. He sat up to reach for his coffee cup on a side table.

Morning was Herb's favorite time. It was the starting gate. No matter how well you'd planned the day, circumstances could immediately turn everything on its head. He loved the unforeseen. It kept you on the edge.

This particular morning had been welcomed with a

fresh pot of coffee, a fat newspaper and a smug sense of satisfaction. The protracted filming had at last been completed and the set struck. The extra day at the stage had added a little more heft to his paycheck. Herb's next job wouldn't start for another week. Which was a good thing because there was some unfinished business to attend to.

No, they'd found nothing at the beach house. But then their search had been interrupted when they heard the Jeep pull in. Oops, sorry. Have to run. Bye. Don't worry. We'll be back for another stab. Oh, he liked that analogy. Stab. Clever boy. But they would indeed return to Mr. Jack Hunter's residence for a second look around. And this time they'd be ready for any surprises.

~~~

"You can buy a human skull on the net," Tom Bradshaw said. "On eBay, for God's sake! What makes you believe this thing didn't come from Nigeria or someplace?"

The detective was talking with Dalton and Rivers at the homicide table. Dalton had returned from the county morgue.

"That's a consideration," Dalton agreed. "But the ME thinks the skull and the hands belonged to the same person. I'm not certain you could find that kind of match on the net. It'd be a long shot for sure. Besides, the Biotex trace on both the skull and hands seems to tie them together, wouldn't you say?"

"What *I'd* say is it is interesting," Bradshaw smiled, "but whether there's a connection or not remains to be seen."

"I would agree, boss," Dalton said. "Except that this poor bastard had his head and hands removed by a novice with an axe and I can't see Biotex being a staple in Nigeria."

Bradshaw shot her a look.

"Wasn't there a case involving some bones and a skull in Pasadena awhile back?" Rivers asked.

"Yeah," Bradshaw yawned. "Some mumbo jumbo about a cult ritual. Nothing substantial ever came of it, as far as I can remember. No crime committed anyway."

"Here's something interesting," Rivers smiled. "I meant to tell you this when you came in, Laura. Anyway, this morning I was at roll call and the sergeant showed this picture of a missing person to patrol. I grabbed a copy."

He pulled a folded piece of paper from his pocket and showed it to Dalton.

"Isn't that the guy who was with your friend at the shooting on Mulholland?"

Dalton scrunched her eyes and scanned the printout.

"He *does* look familiar," she said, handing it back.

"And why were you at roll call this morning, Rivers?" Bradshaw asked, turning to the young detective.

"I like to do that every once in awhile, sir," Rivers said, blushing. "Gives me a picture of what's up in the division for the day. Carryover from when I was on patrol."

"Uh, huh, we can put you back on patrol if that's some kind of heart's desire of yours," Bradshaw grinned.

"No, sir, I'm happy here."

"Well, just stay out of the sergeant's way," Bradshaw said, then abruptly, "I have a meeting downtown. See you later."

He left the two detectives sitting at the homicide table. After a moment, Dalton stood up.

"Let's go have a talk with the watch commander."

Buz Rossman was a 20-year veteran with the LAPD with a rocker supporting his three stripes which meant he was a Sergeant II. He'd worked at Van Nuys for the past five, having spent a couple of lifetimes at the tough Southeast Division before that. He was street cop to the core and a no-nonsense guy.

"What can I do for you, detectives?" he grumbled.

"Understand you handed out a missing person sheet this morning," Dalton answered, forgoing any niceties.

"Favor to the Mounties," he said, using his nickname for the Sheriffs.

"Detective Rivers here thinks he may have seen the missing man. Do you have anything more on him?"

Rossman cut his eyes at Rivers.

"Sheriffs responded to a DB in a burned car. VIN number showed the car belonged to a Mike Eaton in Sherman Oaks. Asked us to verify the address. Nobody at home."

Dalton felt something dark stir.

"Oh, one more thing," Rossman said, holding up a finger. "Patrol reported another person at the address. Supposedly a friend of the owner. Identified himself as Jack Hunter. Nothing suspicious."

Here we go, Dalton thought to herself.

CHAPTER 10

"Funny, I was about to call you," Jack said into his phone. He'd been exiled to the deck. The technicians were busy inside installing the new security system.

"You were at Mike Eaton's house yesterday." Dalton got right to the point. "True?"

She was still at the Van Nuys station.

"Uh, yeah, I hadn't heard back from him after calling about a zillion times, so I was worried and drove by. The cops were there, too. What's up?"

"I'm not sure but Mike could be in trouble."

Trouble as in *dead* passed through her mind but she didn't say it to him.

"Do you know anything about Mike?" she asked. "I mean, personally. Was he into weird stuff, for instance?"

Jack laughed. A couple strolling along the beach waved at him. He returned it.

"I never asked about his personal life," he said, "but as far as I could tell, he wasn't a kook. Why are you asking?"

"Are you going to be home for awhile?"

"I've got a house full of techies. They kicked me out while they installed a new security system. Some jerk broke in the other night."

"Broke in? Why didn't you tell me? Look I need to talk with you. I'll be there as soon as I can get away from here. Don't leave."

She ended the call and turned to Rivers.

"Hold down the fort, Jason. I'm going to be out for awhile. Check with the sheriffs and find out the latest they have on that missing person. Probably too early for an autopsy report on the dead man but call the ME anyway. If anyone there gives you any grief about it belonging to the sheriffs, tell 'em it concerns a connecting case. "

~~~

It was heads or tails which would be the quicker drive to Malibu – the 101 to Topanga or over the 405 to Sunset? Normally, Topanga Canyon would've been the hands-down choice but there'd been a small rockslide just the other side of Fernwood. She wasn't sure it'd been cleared so Sunset won the toss.

As usual the 405 was a nightmare but once she got to Sunset Boulevard, it was a breeze to the Pacific Coast Highway. She whipped the Porsche into Jack's drive and parked next to the security company's van.

"Can I get you a cup of coffee, coke or anything?" Jack asked.

They'd gone out onto the deck to get away from the hubbub inside.

"I'm good, thanks. So tell me about the break-in."

Right then one of the technicians stuck his head out of the door.

"Won't be much longer, Mr. Hunter," he reported. "Have to run a couple of tests and that's it."

" Wow, these guys look like they're wiring up the CIA," Dalton said. "Is that a TV monitor he's carrying upstairs?"

"It goes in the bedroom," Jack explained. "There's another in the kitchen. All the rooms have cameras hooked up in sequence so you can see on the screens what's happening throughout the whole house. Around the outside, too. Once it's armed and a problem is spotted, the system notifies the security company and tells the cops to come a-running."

"Slick," Dalton noted. "Back to the break-in, was anything taken?"

"Nothing that I could tell. Odd, huh?"

Dalton paused.

"Jack, could this break-in be related to the car you just

bought?" she asked thoughtfully. "Not the car itself, but that box. I know I'm reaching but hear me out."

She then told him about her visit to the medical examiner that morning and recounted everything Jason had earlier discovered.

"But your boss said anyone could buy a human skull," Jack argued. "So what's so special about the one in the box? Could've come from Walmart."

He involuntarily added a goofy grin. An old habit whenever he felt under pressure. And one that never failed to dig him in deeper.

"Remember what I just told you about the marks on the bones?" she said, ignoring the grin, which in the past had always irked her. "Whoever beheaded that person and amputated the hands wasn't a surgeon."

Jack let that settle for a moment. Recent news stories of terrorists streamed through his mind.

"That doesn't mean it happened here." he said. "Some middle eastern countries hack off heads and hands with regularity. We don't know where the things came from."

Dalton took in a long breath. The couple on the beach that had earlier passed by came back. Jack gave another small wave. It wasn't returned.

"Not very friendly people," Dalton observed. "Neighbors?"

"I don't care about the damn bones," Jack said. "But I am worried about Mike. He's still not answering his phone. I checked with his office again and they've had no word. And no, they aren't neighbors as far as I know."

"I have to tell you there was a body found in Mike's car," Dalton said. "The Sheriffs' detective division is investigating."

A shocked expression came to Jack's face.

"The cops didn't mention that when they came to his house," he said quietly.

"The Sheriffs don't know the identity of the body and the medical examiners office hasn't done an autopsy yet. Doesn't mean it's Mike."

Jack turned and looked out to sea.

"I'm sorry, Jack."

"Want to drive over to Century City and talk with Brenda?" he suggested. "She runs Mike's office."

"I would be overstepping my bounds," Dalton told him. "This belongs to the sheriffs office. But I can call them and give their investigator Brenda's name and number. I'm sure they'll eventually get to her. That could speed things up a bit."

Jack heaved a breath.

"It's Brenda Carson," he said, checking his smartphone for the number. "The company is Eaton Classic Cars at 213 854-6284. Mike wasn't a close friend or anything like that. He was just a good guy. I enjoyed being around him."

"Does he have any children?" she asked, jotting down the information.

"Think he's got a son living somewhere. Oregon, yeah."

"What about his wife?"

"Never mentioned her. Don't know if he's divorced, widowed or what. Brenda might know."

The guy from the security office came out onto the deck.

"We're ready to show you how to work your new system, Mr. Hunter."

Dalton took hold of Jack's hand.

"I've got to go back to the office," she said. "I'll talk to the sheriffs. You take care, all right?"

Dalton hadn't been gone for more than a minute when Jack's phone beeped. He didn't recognize the number.

"Yeah?" he answered.

"Is this Jack Hunter?" a voice asked.

"That's right. Who are you?"

"This is Dave Hudson. I have a radio show in town and I'm doing a story concerning some bones including a human skull the police recently found which may be tied to an unsolved homicide. I understand that you were in possession of them, is that correct?"

Jack's mouth dropped open.

"I don't know anything about a homicide," he said. "What was your name again?"

"Dave Hudson. You must've heard of my show, Weird Dave? You starred on it once, remember? I kept the public up to date when you were suspected of killing your wife. Seems that kind of thing follows you around, huh? Now according to my information, the bones were being kept in a very special container when the police discovered them. Why did you keep them in there, Mr. Hunter? Where did you get them? By the way, I'm recording our conversation."

Jack had to laugh. It was deja vu all over again.

"I don't know where your information came from but I can guarantee you it's a load of unadulterated bullshit. But then that's your trade, isn't it. Don't bother me again."

He shut off his phone, knowing that wouldn't be the last of it. The guy was a sleaze. How did he get this stuff?

"Ready when you are, Mr. Hunter," the technician called down.

Jack mounted the stairs to the bedroom.

"Be right with you," he said. "Let me make a quick call."

~~~

"He mumbled something about going to see a possible client," Brenda Carson said tearfully. "I think it was Topanga."

"Did he say who it was?" Jack asked.

Jack had earlier phoned Brenda to ask if she could stay a little later at the office, that he needed to talk. Understanding the new security system had been child's play and he was able to leave sooner than he'd figured.

"Yes, I have it here somewhere," she said, shuffling through some papers. "When the man first called, he said that he was looking for a Jaguar. I gave him to Mike and he made an appointment to see him. Ah, here it is, Aleister Crowley."

"What about an address or number?"

"Mike probably has that in his phone along with the address. A lot of times people aren't really serious when they call here and they don't want to leave their phone number. Probably too embarrassed."

"But you're sure he said he was going to Topanga?"

"I think so," Brenda answered. "He was in a hurry. Said the man had just called again and asked if he could come to his house. This is all so terrible."

Jack smiled. A dead end right at the start.

"I know," he said sympathetically. "Could I buy you a drink or a coffee?"

"No, thanks. I've got a casting callback over on Sunset at 6 o'clock. It's for a national commercial. Big client."

"Hey, that's great! I'll keep my fingers crossed for you."

"Me, too."

~~~

Jack seated himself at the bar in the Bel Air Hotel.

"What are you having, sir?" the barkeeper asked.

"Glass of Merlot, please. House wine's fine."

It'd been quite a while since he had last been here. Sitting alone at the bar, possibly on the same stool, and innocently having a drink when his ex-wife had walked in with another man. Their divorce had been finalized on that very same day. The next day she was dead.

His wine came and he took a sip.

What had drawn him to the hotel tonight, he wondered? Certainly not for old time's sake. It was like his life was resetting. He'd once been suspected of murder. Lived on the fringes in Key West as a fugitive. Found his way back and was cleared of a horrendous crime. Came into a fortune that was still multiplying. And through it all, trouble never seemed to lag more than a footstep behind, arm outstretched and ready to touch him on the shoulder. Now this latest mystery.

Tomorrow he'd drive to Topanga Canyon.

CHAPTER 11

A dust devil danced along the edge of the dry lake, swirling like a miniature twister and disappearing into the surrounding scrub. Thermals shot up from the flat lake surface launching shafts of invisible turbulence.

Nothing stirred, however, where Emilio Zaragoza was standing. He stared at the black smudgy shape on the desert floor.

"You said someone was filming a commercial out here the day before?" he asked Deputy Charles Brinkley.

They'd returned to the location of the burnt vehicle, meeting at the entrance road where the deputy had parked his cruiser and then the two of them had driven out in Zaragoza's Land Rover.

"That's right, sir," Brinkley said. "I have the name of the production company. I'll call for a list of the crew members."

"Good, I may want to talk with them. What about the guy who discovered the car?"

"Name's Wade Davis. He lives near here. Often comes out to scrounge around after a commercial. Kind of a picker, I guess."

"Uh, huh, and he said that he'd noticed the fire the night before?"

"Yes, sir, he thought it had something to do with the filming. Didn't pay it any mind."

"Un-fucking-believable!" Zaragoza muttered to himself.

The detective circled the burned area again. He bent down and examined the hardened ground.

"Notice this white stuff spread around?" he called to Brinkley.

He wet his finger and touched the substance with it.

"Looks like salt," he commented curiously, placing the white crystals on his tongue. "Shit, it is salt!"

"Maybe it leached out of the lake bed," Brinkley offered. "Fire had something to do with it."

"Sounds farfetched but who knows," Zaragoza said, rising to his feet. "Okay, let's get the hell out of here. I've seen enough."

Like many cops, Zaragoza always returned to the scene of a crime he was investigating. Every now and then you'd learn something new. The curious salt ring aside, this hadn't been one of those times.

"I'm driving to Santa Monica after I drop you off," he said to Brinkley as the Land Rover smoothed out the bumps. "Talk with Mike Eaton's secretary."

Dalton had phoned the Homicide Bureau the evening before and had finally gotten ahold of Zaragoza. He'd thanked her for the information but said that he already had the woman's name.

"You're pretty sure he's the victim, huh?" Brinkley said.

"He's the best one we have so far."

Brinkley laughed.

"How're your boys?" he asked.

"Robert's been accepted at West Point," Zaragoza said with a smile. "Owe one to the congressman for that. And Philip is starting his second year at UC Davis. Thinking of becoming a vintner."

"You must be proud," Brinkley said.

"Yeah, I am. Their mom would've been, too."

~~~

Jack pulled into the small shopping center between the villages of Topanga and Fernwood. Not too long ago the little wooded community of Topanga in Los Angeles County was a hippie enclave running all the way to the ocean and ending on a surfer's beach. But the Age of Aquarius had moved on and now it was more of a haven for artists, writers, spent musicians and aging film stars. He found a parking space in front of a coffee shop and went inside.

"I'll have a double espresso," he said to the barista, a young girl who looked to be home on a college break.

"Our single shots are like doubles," she smiled. "You still want a double?"

"I'll go with your recommendation," Jack smiled back.

A couple of customers were engrossed in their laptops. Another, a man maybe a little older than Jack, sat reading a newspaper. He seemed a friendly sort and Jack took his espresso over to table next to him.

"Great morning, huh?" Jack commented.

The man looked up.

"Yeah, but it's going to be a hot one," he said. "Unless you're at the beach."

"My next stop," Jack chuckled. "Malibu."

"That where you live?"

"Checking out some property," Jack told him, which wasn't a lie since he was going home. He had dressed in a smart black sports coat and a pair of jeans.

"Oh, so you're in real estate?"

"It buys the groceries," Jack laughed.

"Well, it'd pay for the whole damn supermarket if you're selling in Topanga. The housing market's off the charts. I can't imagine what it must be like in Malibu."

"How about you?" Jack asked. "Live around here?"

"Born and raised in Topanga. My parents moved to the canyon in the early sixties. Missed the love-fest in Haight-Ashbury so they grabbed the next best. They recently passed and now I have their place."

Jack gave a nod.

"Maybe you can help me," he said. "I'm trying to find a

person who lives in the area that may be looking to sell. Got a lead on him from an associate but no address."

"What's his name?"

"Aleister Crowley. You know him?"

The man scrunched up his face.

"I don't believe so. Crowley, you say?"

"Yeah, Aleister Crowley. Spells his first name a-l-e-i-s-t-e-r. Kind of unusual."

"Nope. Tell you what, leave me your card and I'll ask around."

"Thanks. That'd be terrific."

Jack took out a business card and handed it to the man.

"Jack Hunter ... The Pamela Company," he read, holding it at arm's length. "My name's Bill Evans."

"Glad to meet you, Bill. You wouldn't be interested in listing your house, would you?"

"Don't think so. Once you move out, you can't afford to get back in."

Jack thanked him again and got up to leave.

"You might ask about that address at the bookshop a couple of doors down," Evans suggested.

The bookshop was named Xanadu and had a little bell above the door that tinkled whenever anyone came in. A tall, attractive lady dressed in jeans and a tank top smiled at Jack and then returned to sorting books on a shelf.

"Let me know if I can help you find anything," she said.

"Just browsing," Jack told her.

It wasn't a large place. Long and narrow with books displayed on a center counter and along either wall. To the rear was another counter and a glass case filled with crystals, geodes and handmade jewelry. There was also a small section for incense sticks, oils and sage bundles. And yet another room farther back held more merchandise.

New Age music tinkled in the background.

Jack wandered around, picking up a book for a quick peruse and then replacing it. Most of the covers were by popular authors, some on the bestseller lists, but a few local writers were also present. Mysteries, thrillers, even a section on the occult. He stopped there.

"Find something you like?" the woman asked.

"No, just curious," Jack said. "I do have a question though. Do you know a person who lives around here named Aleister Crowley?"

The woman gave him an odd look.

"Is this a joke?"

"Seriously," Jack said. "Has a funny way of spelling his first name."

"I know how it's spelled. Aleister Crowley had probably the greatest influence on Satanism in the country. Are you interested in him? I can get you some of his books."

"Only in where he lives," Jack said excitedly. "It's important that I talk with him. Can you give me his address?"

"Go to hell," she laughed.

"I beg your pardon?"

"He died in 1947. My guess is you'll find Aleister Crowley dead and well in hell today."

Jack looked at her for a second and then laughed himself.

"You won't believe this," he said, "but I did Google his name. Yeah, he was everything you said. I just thought someone here had the same name."

"Well, I have to admit it was funny," the woman said. "My name's Alison. No relation to Aleister."

"I'm Jack. Do you own this place?"

"Lock, stock and barrel. Bell, book and candle, too. I'd give you a business card but I'm out and the printer hasn't delivered the new ones."

Jack gave her one of his.

"Take mine," he said. "If a living Aleister Crowley walks in, please call me."

CHAPTER 12

The three strips of fused duct tape wrapped around the lower part of the head gave the appearance of a steel jaw. It was carefully removed with forceps and placed in a bowl. Forensics would later examine the adhesive side for fingerprints.

"I'm going to make a Y-incision now," Dr. Sally Davis announced.

The corpse lay on a steel table at the LA County morgue. An internal examination starts with a deep incision made from shoulder to shoulder to the breastbone and then extends down to expose the organs.

Davis had recently joined the Medical Examiners Office. This was her first autopsy. John Logan had joined her in the suite.

"I think we can get prints from his left hand," he said. "Also, we need a shot of the teeth to check against dental charts, if they become available."

"Jesus, one of his fingers has been cut off," Logan muttered. "Damn fire didn't do that."

~~~

Emilio Zaragoza introduced himself to Brenda Carson. He'd stopped by his home in Santa Clarita on the way back from the desert to exchange his worn jeans and scuffed cowboy boots for a tan worsted suit, a light blue shirt and dark brown shoes.

"Thanks for seeing me," he said, adding a warm smile.

"I only hope I can help," she smiled back nervously. "Have you found anything? I mean, you know."

"The car contained a deceased male," Zaragoza stated factually.

Brenda's eyes widened.

"Oh, Lord! Do you think it's Mike?"

"We won't know that until we get a positive identification. Also, I ask that you keep this to yourself. But if you could tell me a little about Mr. Eaton it might be helpful."

"Well, I really don't know all that much," Brenda said. "I mean, he's kind of private."

"Do you know if he's married?" Zaragoza asked. "I haven't found any mention of a wife."

"Mike is gay. He was married at one time and has a son. In Oregon, I think. I don't know about the ex-wife. Mike told me all this when I came to work for him."

Zaragoza nodded.

"Does he have a partner?"

"Sam Purdy. They met soon after Mike came out. He died three months ago. Mike's still in bereavement."

"Losing someone close is tough," he said. "Takes a while to get used to it. What about friends? Did he have many?"

"I don't know. Maybe when Sam was alive. But clients are the only people I've seen him with."

"Any client in particular stick out?"

"Not really. But the last one was nice. They got along well. In fact, he's also concerned about Mike. He came by yesterday to see if I'd heard anything."

"You have his name?" Zaragoza asked.

"Jack Hunter. He lives near Malibu. Mike recently found him a car. It was a Jaguar XKE."

"Is he a car collector? This Jack Hunter fellow?"

"I don't think so. Collectors go for the high-end stuff you see at the big auctions. Like up in Monterey. Mike occasionally works with one or two of them. But mostly he deals with people looking for something special they can drive on the weekend."

"You have an address on Hunter?" Zaragoza asked.

"Sure, I'll get it for you. Mike was proud of the Jaguar he found for him. Came from an estate here in town. Coincidentally, another person was interested in the same car and wanted to buy it from Mr. Hunter. Mike was supposed to see him but apparently he never did."

Zaragoza's heart rate slowed, his breathing evened out. It always happened at times like this. Whenever coincidences cropped up. He didn't believe in coincidences.

"How about that other person?" he asked. "The one who was also interested in the car. You remember his name?"

Brenda gave a little laugh.

"Aleister Crowley," she said. "Spells his first name a weird way. Oh, and I think Mike said he lived in Topanga, but I'm not sure about that."

~~~

Highway 14 split off the Interstate 5 and ended at the desert community of Mojave. On the way it passed the road to Acton, a dot on the map north of Los Angeles where George Overton had a home with his second wife.

George was a cameraman and enjoyed steady work with several production companies filming television commercials. Not only did he possess a good eye but also a strong editorial sense. He knew if one scene was going to work with another or not. Directors often depended on George's judgment. Most thought he was a fun guy to have around, too. Very personable and got along well with the crew.

In short, he was the last person you'd expect of being a Satanist. His first wife, Beth, certainly hadn't. She'd thought he was the most goodhearted God-fearing man on earth. A straight arrow with solid Christian beliefs and sent to her with Heaven's blessings. She'd been lucky to get out of the marriage with her life intact. And any blessing that came with the unholy union was that it hadn't produced a child. Beth moved to Florida and never looked back.

The second wife, Cassandra, had stepped into his life with eyes slightly more open. She was a Goth and had ties with a couple of cults. They'd sometimes perform animal sacrifices and dabbled in Satanism. George introduced her to the real thing.

"I can't get away tonight, Herb," he said. "Cass's birthday."

George had been in the middle of restringing a guitar for a neighbor when Thacker called. He belonged to a small group of musicians that played on weekends at a bar in Palmdale.

"Maybe tomorrow," he said.

"It has to be tonight," Herb insisted. "He won't expect us."

"Then you'll have to do it without me."

"I'm planning a mass," Herb spat angrily. "I've found a new place for us. We need that repository. For all we know, that fool might've opened it."

"There's no way he can without the key," George countered.

"What if he breaks into it?" Herb shouted. "He could damage the skull!"

"I still can't get away tonight."

"Remember your vows, George," Herb said quietly. "I also remind you that we alone are responsible for our actions."

"Don't get sanctimonious with me, Herb. It's not in your best interest."

"I'm in a bind, George. Help me out."

Overton gave a little snort.

"I'll see what I can do," he said.

~~~

"Laura, this is Francine Mason, remember me?"

Dalton was at her desk in detectives. She'd been just about to call the Medical Examiners office when her phone rang.

"Of course I do, Francine," she said happily. "How are you and what're you up to?"

Mason had been a reserve officer at West LA when Dalton was a detective 1 in homicide. She had since gone back to the academy to become a regular with the LAPD. She now worked patrol in Hollywood.

"Still driving around Hollyweird protecting and serving," Mason said. "Speaking of weird, that's why I'm calling. Do you remember that Weird Dave character who has the talk radio show? He was involved in a case you worked at West LA."

"I remember who you're talking about but I don't listen to him."

"Well, I do. Secret vice, I guess. Anyway, he mentioned your friend last night on his show."

"What? Who?"

Mason laughed.

"Jack Hunter, silly!"

Dalton's memory flashed back to that earlier case. The victim had been Pamela Ridenour, a wealthy real estate investor, and the person-of-interest in the investigation was her ex-husband, Jack Hunter, who was on the run. Weird Dave had a guest who was in touch with Jack and blabbed misinformation all over the air.

"What did Weird Dave say?" she asked apprehensively.

"Something about your friend having a human skeleton that could belong to an unsolved homicide victim. Oh, and how Jack had once been a murder suspect."

~~~

Jack had driven back to his house and was relaxing on

the deck with a book. Among the odds and ends that'd come with the car, he'd discovered a bound collection of articles written by automotive experts about the Jaguar E Type. It would make fascinating reading for an engineer. Still, there were great photographs, schematic drawings, performance charts, old advertisements and most startling, the price of a new XKE at that time. Six thousand dollars.

A woman wearing a bikini and a shear beach robe walked past at the water's edge carrying an empty wine glass. Jack was verging on calling out with an offer to refill the glass when his cell phone rang. The ID showed it was Eric Nystrom.

"Mr. Nystrom, thank you for returning my call," Jack answered.

"You're welcome. I got your pictures. My question is, how far do you want to go with the restoration?"

Jack had earlier e-mailed him some photos of the Jaguar.

"I'm thinking of the car as more of a driver," he said. "So what I'm looking for is getting it mechanically straight. There's no rust as far as I can tell and the paint looks good. All the chrome is bright. Even the canvas top hasn't rotted."

"Uh-huh, and you want to drive it, you say?"

"Yes, I was planning to ... unless something's wrong with that, is there?"

"No, it's just that your car might be worth more by not driving it."

Jack sighed.

"I'm not sure I'm following you," he said.

"A collector would want to keep the car as original as possible," Nystrom explained. "I mean down to the tires. There's a class in car shows for this. Becoming a big deal these days."

Jack mulled that over.

"Well, I can see now where you're coming from but I don't know," he said.

"Tell you what, I have an associate up in Ventura who can come look at the car," Nystrom offered. "He can give you his opinion and then you can decide what you want to do."

"I've never even tried to start the engine," Jack said. "Think he could check it out?"

"Absolutely. I'll give him a call today."

The woman carrying the empty wine glass passed by again. This time a man was with her. Both looked toward Jack's house and began walking across the beach to it.

~~~

Detective Zaragoza had come up empty-handed after leaving Century City. His department had found no listing for an Aleister Crowley in Topanga. He'd decided to drive there anyway and ask around. Afterwards, he could drop in on Hunter.

There wasn't that much to see in the canyon. He came to a small shopping center. A bookstore looked promising.

"Hi," he said to the tall and attractive lady inside.

"Hi, yourself," she said back, smiling. "Can I help you with something?"

Zaragoza blushed. His reaction surprised him.

"Yes," he said, pulling out his ID. "I'm with the LA County Sheriffs and I'm trying to run down a guy name Aleister Crowley. Suppose to live around here."

"I knew it was a joke!" she laughed. "Are you for real? C'mon, you can let me in on it."

This place was becoming full of surprises, Zaragoza thought.

"No, ma'am, I'm not here for a joke," he said seriously.

Now it was Alison's turn to blush

"I'm sorry. My name is Alison Gordon. I own the shop."

Zaragoza lightened up. She was awfully attractive.

"Emile Zaragoza," he said. "You asked if I was joking. Was there something funny I said?"

Alison took a deep breath.

"You're really serious about Aleister Crowley, aren't you? Well, he doesn't live around here. In fact, he died half a century ago."

"You're kidding," Zaragoza said in disbelief. "His name was mentioned in a homicide investigation."

Alison took a step back and looked at him quizzically.

"Crowley was a Satanist," she said. "Not someone you'd want to know. But here's something really funny. You're the second person to come in here and ask about him."

~~~

"Hello, partner, wonder if we could trouble you for a drink of water," the man called up to Jack.

He and the bikinied woman stood on the sandy beach below Jack's deck.

"Girlfriend and I have walked damn near to Mexico and back," he continued with a laugh. "Feeling a little parched."

The girlfriend wasn't bad looking, Jack noticed, now that she'd come closer. A little on the scary side, though. Dark hair. Her eyes had a feral expression. Not that being a wild woman was a bad thing, as far as he was concerned. She held up the empty wine glass and smiled.

"Sure," Jack said. "Wait a minute. I'll get you a couple of bottles of water."

Jack went inside to his kitchen and opened the refrigerator. He grabbed the bottled water and turned to find that the couple had come up onto the deck and were now standing in the living room.

"I'm George," the man said, putting out his hand. "This is Cass."

Jack felt Cass might spring at him at any moment.

"I thought I told you to wait," Jack said sharply, ignoring the handshake. "I didn't invite you in."

"Sorry, man, didn't mean to overstep any boundaries here," George apologized. "Hey, are those your horns? Okay if I take a look? I got a little band I play in myself."

Jack was caught short by the man's brashness.

"Nice place you got," George commented, taking in the room while walking over to the saxophones. "Live here by yourself?"

Nosey bastard as well as being rude, Jack thought as that little warning light began to flicker in the back of his mind. He sized up his new guest. The man was a lanky sort, hair going to iron-gray and slightly longish. The woman gave off a bad vibe.

"So you're a musician, huh?" George grinned, jamming his hands into his jeans pockets and letting his fingers slide over the handle of a knife. A faint smile curled the corners of Cass's lips.

The doorbell rang.

"Excuse me while I get that," Jack said and turned away.

Cass shot George an anxious look. George had slipped the knife out of his pocket and flicked open the five-inch spear-pointed blade but Jack was already at the door, his hand on the knob.

"Los Angeles County Sheriffs Department," Zaragoza announced when the door opened. "I'm Detective Emilio Zaragoza. Are you Jack Hunter?"

"I am," Jack answered. "But I've already talked to you guys."

"Beg pardon?"

"About the break in. Nothing was taken and I've

upgraded my security. So how can I help you?"

"Do you know a Mr. Mike Eaton?" Zaragoza asked.

"Yes," Jack answered, a note of anxiety in his voice. "He's been missing. Do you have some news? Come in. I've got a couple of people inside but they're leaving."

The two men walked into the living room. It was empty. The door to the deck stood open.

"Nice place," Zaragoza commented.

Jack hurried out onto the deck but could see no one on the beach. He returned inside.

"Your friends seem to have left."

"They weren't friends," Jack said, somewhat unsettled. "So you have some information about Mike, huh?"

"Do you live here alone, Mr. Hunter?"

"That's the second time I've been asked that in the past five minutes," Jack said suspiciously. "Both times by strangers, too. What the hell does that have to do with anything?"

"I not sure I understand what you're talking about, sir."

Jack took a deep breath and exhaled.

"There was a couple here just now," he said. "Walked up while I was out on the deck and asked me for a drink of water. When I went to get it for them, they came inside. Guy wanted to know if I were alone. "

"Not a good practice to invite strangers into your home," Zaragoza said.

"I didn't invite them," Jack explained. "They followed me inside after I told them to wait. Thing is, I was getting a bad vibe off of them when you rang the doorbell. Tall guy. Girl had cat eyes. But to answer your question, yes, I live here alone."

"Are you gay, Mr. Hunter?"

Jack looked at him strangely.

"Is that a proposition you're making?" he asked.

"Not at all. Mr. Eaton was gay. I was wondering if the two of you had a relationship."

Jack had to laugh at that.

"Actually, I didn't know that Mike was gay. We did have a business relationship, though. He found a car for me. He's an all right kind of guy. Pleasant to be around. As to the other, no, I'm not gay. I'm a widower. My wife died a couple of years ago. She was a female, by the way."

"I'm sorry," Zaragoza said. "I understand. I lost my wife a few years back."

"Zaragoza ... interesting name," Jack said. "Wouldn't be related to any Ranzoas, are you?"

"Don't think so."

"Just wondering," Jack smiled. "Family I knew in Florida were named Ranzoa. Down in Key West."

"Never been there."

"So what is it about Mike that you want to know?" Jack asked.

"A car registered to him was found in the desert. There was a dead body inside. We haven't made positive identification yet but we believe it may be Mr. Eaton."

Jack walked over to a chair and sat down.

"What kind of car?" he asked, motioning at a chair for the detective. "Please, have a seat."

"Honda Accord," Zaragoza said, continuing to stand.

"Mike drives an Accord. What's the holdup on the identification?"

"The body was badly burned."

"I'm getting the impression that it wasn't Mike's doing, that right?"

"We believe it's homicide."

"Ah, fuck!"

Zaragoza sat down.

"You were asking about an Aleister Crowley at a bookshop in Topanga," he continued. "What is your connection with Crowley?"

"Christ, how'd you know about the bookshop?" Jack said, shaking his head in amazement. "Guess you must have been taken in by this Aleister Crowley character, too. Anyway, Mike's girl, Brenda Carson, she runs the office, mentioned that he was seeing someone by that name the day he disappeared. He'd called Mike wanting to buy the Jag that he'd found for me but Mike told him that I wasn't interested in selling. Mike was going to show him some other cars."

Zaragoza nodded. He decided to remove Jack Hunter from his persons-of-interest list. However, he wasn't certain where to place him instead just yet.

"So you were trying to find Crowley," he said. "Why?"

"I was worried about Mike. Brenda said that he was driving to the guy's house in Topanga. She didn't have an address. Just a name. I asked around a couple of places in Topanga, including the bookshop. Apparently you did too."

"What's so special about this car of yours?" Zaragoza asked.

Jack smiled.

"It's an old Jaguar XKE," he said. "Always wanted one but now I wish I hadn't gotten the thing. You obviously know about the skull since you're here."

"A detective with the LAPD called us," Zaragoza said. "Filled me in."

"That must've been Laura Dalton. She's a friend."

CHAPTER 13

"I want to get a forensic team to dig around at that greenhouse," Dalton said to Bradshaw. "Maybe a cadaver dog, too."

She and the detective were sitting at the homicide table.

"You really think there's something there?" he asked.

"I think something happened there. Whether it is still there or not, we need to find out."

"We'd have to get a search warrant," Bradshaw told her. "And then suppose it's a bust? The department could be open to legal action. You know how it is today. Also, it might be more difficult for the court to grant another warrant."

"Yeah," Dalton sighed. "I know, I know. But you weren't at the scene. You didn't smell that awful odor. It was ungodly."

Bradshaw sat quietly for a moment.

"You mentioned earlier that a lot of animal skeletons were inside the house," he said. "Maybe they were skinned or whatever out there. I don't know what the shelf life is on stink but there's no reason to believe what you smelled belongs to a human."

"It was strong, Tom."

"Could be that goat," Bradshaw joked, then seriously, "Laura, we don't have probable cause here."

"I know, it's just a hunch, Tom. But don't tell me you haven't gone out on a limb before with a hunch."

Bradshaw laughed.

"Okay, how about this?" he offered. "We both go there tomorrow morning and look around. Just by ourselves. Say there are still some questions regarding the shooting, if anybody needs to know."

"Sounds good," Dalton said. "It'd be great if we could grab a few soil samples."

"Don't even think about it, Laura."

Vic Young walked into the detectives room. He spotted Dalton and Bradshaw and came over to the table.

"Good afternoon," he greeted them with a broad grin. "Got some info back on that lock. It's a high security piece like I said. This particular one was sold right here in the good old Valley. Kramer Locksmiths on Reseda Boulevard. The owner even remembered installing it."

Dalton took interest in that.

"He didn't happen to remember the customer's name by any chance, did he?" she asked eagerly.

"Yeah, think it's here written down somewhere," Young said, slapping at his pockets. "Must've lost it."

"You didn't!" Dalton cried out.

"Just kidding. Can you say Martin Hodges?"

"Ah, just as we suspected but thanks for verifying."

"Did he remember anything special about Hodges?" Bradshaw asked.

"Said he wasn't a pleasant fellow," Young told him. "Said he was a total asshole, to put it mildly.

"What about the camera case?" Dalton wanted to know. "Was it fitted with the foam cutouts?"

"He didn't say and I didn't ask him," Young replied. "Sorry."

"My guess is that it wasn't," Bradshaw said. "Not really important anyway."

"Thanks, Vic," Dalton smiled. "Appreciate the help."

~~~

George and Cass had ducked beneath the next-door neighbor's deck to hide after hastily exiting. When they were certain that Jack had gone back inside, they had trotted down the beach to the public access where they had left their car.

"Talk about timing," George laughed as they now drove along Topanga Canyon. "Herb's gonna have a cow. Start in about how we should've gone there last night. I almost hate to call him."

"I wanted to see the look on that pig fucker's face when you stuck him," Cass pouted.

"Yeah, baby, but there's always the next time."

Cass giggled and laid her head down in George's lap.

~~~

Emilio Zaragoza was nearly to Santa Clarita when his car phone rang. He saw it was Brinkley.

"What you got for me, Charles?"

Deputy Brinkley was applying to the Sheriffs Detective Bureau. Zaragoza had taken him under his wing.

"ME sent the autopsy on the desert DB," he said.

"Give me a quick digest."

"Poor guy died in the fire. He'd been gagged with duct tape plastered over his mouth. Also, his hands and legs were cuffed with plastic tie-offs which melted but he was probably already dead by then. Finger on one hand had been cut off. Couple of ribs broken pre-mortem. Doc says the fractures could be the result of him struggling in the fire but believes they were caused by someone beating him."

"Identification confirmed?"

"Thumb print from DMV shows he's Michael Eaton."

"Okay, Charles. I'm about home. I'll see you in the office tomorrow."

Zaragoza hung up. He made a mental note to call Detective Laura Dalton at Van Nuys LAPD first thing in the morning. Topanga Canyon was becoming a place of interest in this crime, too. He'd pay Alison Gordon at the bookshop another visit. The question was would it be more for work or pleasure? He smiled at the thought.

CHAPTER 14

The California State DNA Data Bank has been in operation since 1994 and contains nearly two million DNA samples, adding around 25,000 new listings each month. One such sample belonged to Alvis Hume, a convicted felon released from Corcoran State Prison in 2008 after serving three years for burglary. Mr. Hume's DNA had been submitted to the database for previous convictions. It now matched the sample Dr. John Logan had extracted from a tooth in the skull.

"Alvis Hume, a punk who ought to still be inside the slammer," Bradshaw fumed. "Would've been better off if he hadn't been paroled."

"At least his outstanding warrant for parole violation is cleared," Dalton said.

Bradshaw nearly choked on his coffee.

"That's pretty funny," he said. "Better check with his parole officer, too. Also, we might want to run the computer image of his face in the newspaper. See if we get any hits from old friends of his."

"Why not use his booking photo?" Dalton asked.

"I think the one the ME had the techs do looks better. It's close enough to the real thing and there's always something about a booking pix that brings out the crazies."

"What about our warrant to take another look at the Hodges estate?" Dalton asked. "Think we should get one now?"

The two detectives were at the homicide table in Van Nuys. Dalton had just come on duty and had picked up some donuts on the way into the station. Bradshaw, who'd arrived at the station early, quickly polished off the chocolate ones. The ME had emailed the DNA results to

Van Nuys and Bradshaw had then run Hume's arrest record on the computer. It'd been pretty extensive ... robbery, assault with a deadly weapon, burglary, possession of narcotics with intent to sell.

"Not yet," Bradshaw said. "But we sure as hell can take a look around that place. I want to save the warrant for later."

"I just had a thought," Dalton announced. "About those animal skeletons at the house. The medical examiner said that the human skull and hands had been crudely removed. What if the same person who did that also worked on the animals, using the same MO? If so, it would give us more information to work with, maybe help point us where we need to go."

Bradshaw sat silently for a moment mulling that over.

"Know what?" he said at last. "You might have something there. I think now maybe we *should* get that warrant."

Detective Jason Rivers entered the room, a box of donuts tucked under his arm.

"Grab yourself a cup of coffee and get over here," Bradshaw called out. "And take those damn donuts down to patrol."

"You see the paper?" Rivers asked, dropping a copy on the desktop.

~~~

Cass was stretched out on the chaise lounge at the side of the deck, eyes closed while the morning sun played over her nude body. George and Herb sat in chairs across from her sharing the newspaper.

"Hell of a night," George muttered. "Thanks for putting us up. Where's your guest?"

"Still sleeping in," Herb grunted.

George and Cass had decided to tell Herb about the mix-up at Jack's in person rather than over the phone.

They'd stopped at his home in Topanga on the way from Malibu. The news didn't go down well with Herb and one thing had led to another. The last thing being a tremendous amount of wine being drunk.

"You about finished reading that section?" George asked, passing him the sports page. "I'll swap with you."

"That son of a bitch!' Herb exclaimed, ignoring the request. "I knew something like this would happen! Should never have let Sterling go to the house on his own. Guy couldn't find his ass with both hands. Damn!"

Cass rose up on her arms to see what the fuss was all about.

"The goddam cops have the skull!" Herb clamored on. "Son of a bitch! Story about it right here on the last page. That bastard Hunter handed it over to them. Wasn't suppose to go with the car. Fucker robbed us, that's what!"

George snatched the paper from Herb and starting reading the article.

"Now ain't that something," he muttered. "Goes on to say they sent it to the medical examiner, too. Fuck, do you think they can find out anything? Might be a little problem if they do."

Cass had gotten up from the lounge and joined them.

"What's wrong?" she asked, standing next to George. He cupped her pudendum with his hand. She moaned softly.

"Wrong?" Herb sneered. "The whole goddamn world for starters."

"So we were out on a wild goose chase all along," George said. "Our thinking that Hunter character still had the box. It was long gone, probably never in the damn house. If that fucking sheriff hadn't of shown up, it'd sure been his ass. I already had my knife out."

Cass snickered.

"It'd been the biggest surprise of his life," she said.

"Maybe not all is lost," Herb said, now in a calmer mood. "You got inside his house then. We can do it again."

"Nothing there," George pointed out. "No need to go back."

"Oh but there is," Herb grinned. "We need to replace our stolen skull."

"I like that," George laughed. "Your guest can put his awesome talents to work again."

~~~

Sheriffs Detective Zaragoza was at his desk, having just finished reading the entire autopsy report on Mike Eaton when Deputy Brinkley entered the room.

"That production company sent the crew list," he said. "I talked with the owner."

"The who did what?"

"There'd been a film company out there where Eaton was found. Remember?"

"Oh, yeah, of course. My mind was elsewhere."

Indeed, Zaragoza had been completely caught up in the report the medical examiner had written. A chronicle of unimaginable cruelty. Sadly, it wasn't an unfamiliar subject to the detective.

"The name of the outfit is Titan Films," Brinkley said. "They're in Venice Beach. That's down near Santa Monica."

"I know where Venice Beach is," Zaragoza said dryly.

"Yeah, well, mostly they hire freelancers to make the commercials. But some work regularly with them. Then, of course, there's the in-house staff."

Zaragoza leaned back in his chair.

"Sounds confusing," he commented.

"It's the business," Brinkley shrugged.

Zaragoza raised his eyebrows at the deputy, then glanced over the list of names he had given him.

"Christ, how many people does it take to do one of

these things?" he said. "Must be twenty names here."

"Everybody's a specialist, you see," Brinkley explained. "Director, cameraman, assistants up the wahzoo. Think it's a union thing."

Zaragoza sighed.

"All right, then. Since you're the expert, do a run-down on everyone on the crew list. Anything unusual or interesting crops up with anyone, we'll look further into it. Maybe I'll take a drive to their office and talk to the people there."

"Funny thing about that list," Brinkley said. "One name's familiar. George Overton."

Zaragoza sat forward.

"How's that?"

"When I worked West Hollywood, I once answered a domestic violence call. Neighbor had phoned it in. Got to the scene, a small bungalow, and this woman was outside on the sidewalk. Scared to death. Said her husband was in the house and threatening to kill her."

"Had he hit her?" Zaragoza asked.

"Couldn't see any marks. Woman was near panicking. Another unit arrived and I went inside the house to talk to the husband. Of course, he denied everything. Said his wife suffered from paranoia and was always making one thing or the other up."

"How did it end?"

"The usual way. Woman refused to press charges. No signs of physical violence. Told them both if we had to come back somebody was going to jail. George Overton was the husband's name. His wife was Elizabeth. Went by Beth. Pretty blonde lady."

Zaragoza pursed his lips.

"That's amazing," he said. "How the hell do you remember?"

"I kept a personal log of my shifts back then," Brinkley

explained. "Sometimes I read through them. Overton's name rang a bell."

The deputy left the room and Zaragoza picked up his phone and called Dalton at Van Nuys to tell her Eaton had been ID'd. She asked if he could send her a copy of the autopsy report.

After hanging up he decided to call Jack Hunter and let him know. It sounded like the right thing to do. After all, Hunter had known the poor guy.

~~~

Jack sat behind the wood-rimmed steering wheel in the XKE and turned on the ignition key. The warning light activated to standby, the starter button right next to it at the ready. And that was his dilemma. Wait for some ace mechanic to drive down from Santa Barbara or Ventura to push the button. Or just see if the damn thing would run himself.

He had replaced the battery. The engine oil looked clean. He'd even put five gallons of fresh gas in the tank.

He moved his index finger to the starter button and his phone rang.

"Mr. Hunter? This is Sheriffs Detective Zaragoza. How are you, sir?"

"I'm fine, Detective, what can I do for you?"

"I have some unpleasant news, I'm afraid. We have a positive identification. It's Mike Eaton, alright."

~~~

Dalton finished reading the autopsy report. She handed it back to Bradshaw. Rivers was at court walking the warrant through. The Van Nuys Superior Court was only a block from the station. He could easily find a judge to sign off on it.

"Pretty sadistic treatment," Bradshaw commented, putting the report down on the desktop. "Not the worst I've seen but a contender."

"I wonder how he could have made someone angry enough to do that?" Dalton questioned. "Whoever it was went to a lot of trouble to drive him out there. Big risk."

Bradshaw paused over that last comment.

"What makes you think it was risky?" he asked. "Maybe the killers live near the scene. All we know is the victim lived in Sherman Oaks. Could've been visiting somebody out there."

That was an interesting consideration, Dalton thought.

"Suppose they *do* live in the area," she said. "But why drive him out to the middle of nowhere? And then kill him in such a heinous way. Besides the fire could've been seen in the open like that."

"Good question. And one for the Sheriffs to answer. It's their case, remember?"

Dalton acquiesced while weighing the possibilities of her department being drawn into it. Certainly, Bradshaw was correct. It wasn't LAPD's case. But she couldn't escape the feeling that there was a connection between Mike Eaton's murder and that awful skull. There was just that buzz inside her that said so.

She liked Tom and enjoyed working for him. But sometime he could be a little too cautious. Her old boss, Detective Hagen at West LA, would've thrown caution to the wind on a calm day. He could cowboy it when called for. She missed that.

"Tom, I realize the Eaton homicide belongs to the Sheriffs but I also feel that it's somehow tied in with our investigation. Why was James Sterling prowling at the Hodges estate? Next thing, there's a fire in the garage. Then that damn skull shows up. Also, the break-in at Jack Hunter's house. There has to be a connection."

"I'm with you on everything but Hunter's burglary," Bradshaw said. "There's no reason to suspect it had anything to do with the skull. House on the beach at Malibu? C'mon, that's a prime target."

Detective Rivers arrived with the signed warrant.

CHAPTER 15

Jack switched off the ignition, the warning light on the dash immediately died out. He leaned back in the driver's seat and sighed.

"Thank you for letting me know," he said, resuming the conversation with Zaragoza. "I expected that it was Mike. Still, it's kind of a blow."

"It never is not one, sir. There is something you could perhaps help me with, however. A television commercial was being filmed before the incident near the location where the body was found. I have the production company's name and also the advertising agency responsible for it. Gaysome Hoigh. I understand you once worked there, is that right?"

How the hell did he find out that, Jack thought? And what does it matter?

"Yes, I did," Jack told him. "That was some time ago. Why do you ask?"

"This might sound a little strange," Zaragoza said. "But was there anyone you remember there, a co-worker, as being interested in the occult or ever hear any talk about it?"

Jack laughed.

"Do you mean witches and the sort? No, no one wearing a pointed hat, anyway. Creative department was kind of far out but that's always so."

Zaragoza had been intrigued by the ring of salt surrounding the car. He'd researched it and had discovered that salt was often used in occult rituals. This information had given him another path to follow in the investigation. Anyone else would say that he was reaching for straws but once in a while you got one.

"Just a crazy idea, Mr. Hunter," he said humorously. "Sometimes they come to you. Guess it's like your advertising people."

"You said earlier that Mike's car had been found in the desert," Jack remembered. "Could you tell me where? I'd like to see it."

This gave pause to the detective.

"Kind of unusual request, isn't it?" he said. "I'd think most people would want to stay away from where a friend died."

"Yes, Mike was a friend," Jack explained. "Not a close one. But, I don't know, I'd just like to see."

Memories of places where brothers in arms had fallen. Sometimes you returned.

"We consider the area still to be a crime scene, Mr. Hunter," Zaragoza declared. "Once the body is released to the family, I'm sure there will be a funeral and you can pay your respects then."

Jack nodded to himself.

"Well, thanks for letting me know about Mike. Appreciate any updates you can give."

"Will do," Zaragoza said and hung up.

Jack climbed out of the Jag and went to the deck. The Pacific Ocean, blue as a deep lake and devoid of any meaningful surf, lapped meekly along the beach. Not a soul stirred. Not even a breeze. He stood for a moment taking in the scene, then turned to go back inside. Driving the Jaguar was forgotten.

A couple of minutes later he had the information he wanted. He could've gotten it from LA County. The film production company would have pulled a permit from them. But it was quicker to find it on the *Times* website. The crime reporter's article named the location. Turned out Jack had filmed on that same dry lakebed himself back in the day.

~~~

Yellow crime scene tape stretched across the dirt road off the highway that led out to the dry lake. Jack drove around it in the Jeep. Soon he was at the expanse of the lake itself. He stopped and got out.

He'd brought along a compass and a map of the area which he placed on top of the hood. He figured the production company would have scouted the lake for the best position to place the camera. Normally, that would be in the center but not always. He looked at the shape of the lakebed. Oblong with the wider areas being northeast of where he presently stood. That's where he would have chosen had he been producing the commercial. He hopped back in the Jeep and sped out onto the lake, a dusty contrail billowing behind.

Minutes later he was at the location.

The desert floor still held black stains from the fire. Tire tracks crisscrossed the area, some fresher than others. Even a couple of empty plastic water bottles. So much for that pristine crime scene Zaragoza worried over.

Jack picked up the bottles and tossed them in the Jeep to dump later. He then walked over to the blackened shape, a sad document of the unimaginable. The skies rumbled distantly in the altitudes above Edwards Air Force Base.

He had seen enough and turned to leave when he noticed the strange white crystalline ring around where the car had been. He knelt down for a closer look. And like Emilio Zaragoza had earlier done, he put a tiny bit of it on his tongue. Salt.

To the best of his knowledge, salt wasn't normally used as a fire retardant. So what was it doing here? He took out a dollar bill from his wallet and scraped some of the crystals onto it, then folded the bill into a pouch. He might mention it to Laura Dalton. Or he might not.

~~~

Some help from Lucifer was very much needed. Vengeful spirits were circulating since the loss of the skull and seem to be threatening a high priest. This was a serious problem. But Herb Thatcher had come up with a solution.

Taking a chapter out of *The Satanic Bible*, written in the late sixties by Anton LaVey, supposedly a carnival worker in San Francisco, a Mass of Angels would oust the demons.

Herb would need a black bird for the ceremony. He'd found one at a seedy pet shop in the San Francisco Valley, a small crow. The forlorn creature now perched in a makeshift cage out on Herb's deck. For the location, a photographer who had recently filled out the paperwork to join the group, had offered his studio in Santa Monica. Herb didn't want to hold the gathering at his home. George Overton wasn't all that happy about having it at his place either.

Lucifer was the top kick in Hell. He could give or take power. Herb was counting on being given that power tonight. After all, they had named their group after Lucifer's son, Mendes, commonly known as Satan.

The Mendes Society, as it was called, consisted of only a few members. Herb, George, Cass, the photographer as soon as he paid his upfront dues and a high-level priest that had taken over after Martin Hodges had died in the accident and who was now being deviled by the demons. Hopefully, the Society's ranks would increase at an Initiation Mass planned for sometime in the near future. George had a couple of promising prospects on the line. But for the moment all attention was being given to the upcoming ritual.

Oddly, not all followers of Satanism believe in Satan. They're simply atheistic, considering there is neither a literal God nor Satan, and instead look upon Satanism as an alternate to organized religion, for which they share a distinct distaste. Some become activists for separating church from state. Others just like to cause mischief. The Mendes Society, however, is as dark as they come. True believers.

~~~

Titan Films took up most of a corner building facing Venice Boulevard just past US 1. Zaragoza parked in a marked one-hour zone on the side street paralleling the highway and went inside the front door. He found himself in a short hallway. A law firm was at the end. The door on his right indicated a real estate company worked out of it. He chose the one on his left where he saw a pretty girl sitting behind a desk.

"May I help you?" the receptionist flashed a beauty pageant smile when the detective entered.

"Is this Titan Films?" he asked. There'd been no sign on the glass door.

"You win the big prize," she smiled even broader. "The painter guy's redoing the door. He broke for lunch. I'm Sarah."

"I'm with the Sheriffs Department," Zaragoza told her, showing his identification. "I'd like to speak with Brian Gordon. Is he in?"

Sarah's strikingly green eyes teased.

"We've already contributed to the police fund," she said.

"That was very good of you. Now, about Mr. Gordon, is he in?"

"May I ask the nature of your business with him?"

"Crime," Zaragoza smiled.

"Please wait here," Sarah said primly, getting up from her desk. She disappeared down a hallway.

Zaragoza noticed some framed certificates on the wall

and walked over to examine them. Apparently they were some kind of advertising awards. The wall itself was made from distressed wood. On the street side was sandblasted brick. Two large potted palms and a leather sofa made up the furnishings. Sarah's desk was an irregular slab of plate glass balanced on an up-ended automobile racing engine block.

He was starting to feel badly about being a smart-ass with Sarah when she returned with a tall man dressed in expensive jeans and a designer t-shirt.

"Hello, I'm Brian Gordon," he said, sticking out his hand.

The detective took his hand and gave him a quizzical look.

Gordon smiled and cocked his head.

"Is there something wrong?" he asked.

"Oh, I'm sorry," Zaragoza apologized. "It's that I thought I'd seen you before. My name is Detective Emilio Zaragoza. I'm with the LA County Sheriffs Department."

"I don't believe we've met, detective," Gordon said. Then added with a small laugh. "I'm sure I would've remembered anyone from the Sheriffs Department."

"Then you must remember my deputy asking for the crew list on a commercial your company recently filmed at a dry lake."

Gordon looked puzzled.

"I took that call, Brian," Sarah spoke up. "You were out of the office. The officer said they were investigating some kind of crime that happened at the location and were looking for witnesses. I didn't think there was anything wrong with giving it to him. He seemed awfully nice."

Gordon gave her a sharp look.

"That's fine, Sarah," he said. "Perhaps we should go to my office, detective."

Brian Gordon's office wasn't what Zaragoza had

expected. Much smaller and more like a conference room. Painted entirely in red. And there were no windows. Indirect lighting where the walls joined the ceiling. A low highly-polished table sat in the center with four black leather chairs surrounding it. Against one wall was a small workstation with a computer. A huge framed photograph of the 917 Porsche number 23 that won at LeMans covered another wall. That was it.

"Windows distract me when I'm working," Brian Gordon said. He'd noticed Zaragoza giving the room the once-over.

"Please have a seat," he motioned.

Zaragoza sat down facing the picture of the Porsche. Gordon took one of the chairs across from him.

"You must like cars, I guess," Zaragoza said. "I saw that table made from an motor out front. Now this picture."

Gordon beamed.

"Do you know that at one time you could actually buy a Porsche 917 like the one you're looking at and drive it on the street? Of course, you'd have to be crazy. Yeah, I'm kind of a gear head."

"How much would one of those things have cost back then?"

"Oh, 'way north of a hundred thou or so. That 917 in the photograph is now in the Porsche museum. I've seen it."

"A moving experience, I would imagine," Zaragoza smiled again. "What I came here to talk with you about, Mr. Gordon, is the commercial you filmed on the dry lake."

"Yes, that was for an automobile dealership association."

"I see. Did you know that a car was recently found on the very spot where your crew worked only this one had a dead body inside?"

Gordon's mouth dropped slightly open.

"No, I didn't. But I don't see how that has anything to do with my crew. You said it was recently found? It's been a week since the filming."

Zaragoza nodded.

"Oh, I'm not suggesting that the incident involved anyone who worked for you, sir. I was only wondering if someone might've noticed anything unusual at the time of your filming. Such as people hanging around who had no business being there."

"My crew was pretty much in the middle of nowhere," Gordon laughed. "Anyone who was there had a reason to be. But I'll tell you what, I'll check with my director."

"Thank you. What's his name?"

"George Overton. He's a cameraman, as well. Works for us often."

"You have an address for him?"

"Hmm, I think it's somewhere out near Palmdale. I'll ask Sarah. Not sure he's in town right now. Busy guy."

"It would be good if I could have his address."

Zaragoza was interested in how long he had lived that address. Providing he was the same George Overton. And if so, what of his wife? Had she returned?

"Where do you live, Mr. Gordon?" he asked for no particular reason.

"West Hollywood."

"Ah, so you're with us," Zaragoza said.

West Hollywood is an incorporated city within Los Angeles east of Beverly Hills and includes the Sunset Strip. The LA County Sheriffs Department provides general law enforcement to many unincorporated cities and contracts out to incorporated ones.

"Us?" Gordon questioned, tilting his head.

"West Hollywood Station. Where all those Sheriffs cars park."

"Oh, of course," Gordon laughed. "Well, thank you for your service. My wife and I enjoy living there."

"Is your wife also in the film business?"

"Dag is an executive producer for an independent company."

"I would've thought you might have worked together."

"Titan mainly does television commercial and promotional films. Dag's company produces features."

"I see. How long have you two been married?"

"We're just celebrating our first year."

"Congratulations. I would like that address for your cameraman, if you don't mind."

CHAPTER 16

Detectives Dalton and Rivers arrived at the Hodges estate with warrant in hand. They were met by a K9 officer from LAPD who handled a cadaver dog, a medium-sized female of loose lineage. She wore a curly black coat set off with white paws. She had intelligent eyes. Her name was Molly. Paul Tatem was her partner.

"Officer Tatem, glad to see you," Dalton greeted, stepping out of her car. "I'm Laura Dalton and this is Jason Rivers. And who's your friend?"

"This is Molly of the good nose," Tatem said, shaking hands with both detectives.

"Hi, Molly," Dalton said.

Molly ignored her and sat staring straight ahead. All business.

Dalton felt a little affronted by the snub. She had always been kind to animals. She'd taken in that damn cat, hadn't she? So what was up with this snooty pooch?

"What have we got here?" Tate asked.

Dalton explained the case to date, including the fire in the garage and the suspicious marks the ME had discovered on the human bones.

"I'll keep Molly away from the burn area, if that's okay with you," Tatem said when she had finished. "The residual ashes and all are hard on her nose."

"That's fine," Dalton agreed. "Nothing happened in there that we'd need her for, at least to the best of my knowledge. The floor's cement anyway. There's an area behind the main house, though, I'd like for her to check."

"Okay, let's go see what we can find," Tatem said.

The group walked toward the back of the property, Molly on her leash. Along the way, Officer Tatem explained the workings of cadaver dogs.

"Takes a great nose, lots of drive and focus," he said. "Usually start the training when they're puppies. Dogs learn to follow a scent carried in the air or on the ground. Cadaver dogs pick up the smell of human decomposition. There are special chemicals to simulate that for training."

"What does the dog get out of it?" Rivers asked.

"Has to be fun," Tatem smiled. "Biggest thing is the bond between the trainer and the dog. Otherwise it won't work."

"Does it take a specific kind of dog?" Dalton questioned. "I mean, I always thought they used German Shepherds or Labradors, you know, big dogs. Or how about a bloodhound?"

Tatem laughed.

"The jury on which breed is best is still out," he said. "Many different breeds have fine noses. You just have to work with them."

The whole of the San Fernando Valley greeted them when they arrived at the tiny, glass-enclosed structure.

What a view, Dalton thought to herself. If she had a little building like this, she would turn it into something special. Paint the framing a bright color. Wouldn't need electricity, use candles or a lantern. Put down some carpets. Couple of comfortable chairs. That sort of thing. Sit there and watch the Valley in the evenings when all the lights came on and the mountains blackened. It'd be her sanctuary where she could retreat to after working on a shitty case like this present one was turning out to be.

The unpleasant odor tweaked her nose. Not as strong as before. But then the air had been stiller then than now.

"Do you smell that?" Dalton asked Tatem.

"Kind of like manure," he answered. "Maybe chicken poo. My neighbors stink up the whole block when they spread that stuff on their lawns."

"Why don't you let Molly loose?" she suggested.

Tate unclipped the leash and the little cadaver dog trotted off circling the area, nose to the ground.

Dalton expected her to signal at any moment.

~~~

An automobile accident on Malibu Canyon Road just before the state park had traffic at nearly a standstill. Jack decided to turn right on Mulholland and take it to Latigo Canyon Road, which would then take him to the coast highway and home. Mulholland was not only a scenic drive but its twists and turns made it a favorite road course for motorcycles. A couple of Ducati motorcycles whipped around him and dove into the next curve, their riders hunched over the gas tank and practically dragging a knee on the pavement through the turn. He continued on. The open Jeep was kind of like riding a motorcycle, he thought.

Up ahead was the Rock Store, once an old stagecoach stop and now a famous weekend destination for bikers from all over. Today, however, only a couple of motorcycles were standing out front. The two Ducatis. Jack pulled in and parked by the gas pumps, which didn't work and were mainly used as props. Movie scenes were often shot there. He went inside the restaurant and bought a cup of coffee to take out.

Several large logs dragged to the back of the lot served as benches and Jack sat down on one. A pair of scrub jays argued noisily in the brush behind him. One flew away, apparently having had the last squawk. Quiet settled in. Jack let his mind wander.

An inventory of life events seemed in order. He had taken a sabbatical from Key West after the wrenching affair involving the Ranzoas had nearly cost him his sanity. His beach house had become available – short-term tenants – and he'd thought staring at the ocean all day might be good therapy. He'd closed his apartment in Westwood and moved to Malibu.

Things ran smoothly. His business continued to thrive. He and Laura Dalton, while not exactly an item, were nonetheless good friends – well, *he* thought so anyway – and he enjoyed her company. Then came the damn Jaguar XKE.

He had always liked cars and had long ago fallen in love with Jaguar automobiles. They were both beautiful and impossible. And forever beyond reach. Ironically, that summed up all of his relationships. Personal and otherwise.

But fortunes turn. He'd come into considerable money. He'd grown up in a household that had been conservative about spending and he'd kept to that fiscal philosophy himself as an adult. Be that as it may, he could now own any kind of car he desired. So he bought a tricked-out Jeep C5 just for the hell of it. Then the love of his life showed up, a Jag XKE. Unfortunately, now it seemed to have come with a higher price than anyone had expected.

He spotted some business cards and notes pinned on the trunk of a huge oak tree at the side of the parking lot. He went over to examine them.

Several motorcycles for sale. One was a nice-sounding old Triumph. A rock band available for parties. Photographer. Apartment wanted. Free kittens. Xanadu Books.

He took that one down and read it.

Books. Candles. Herbs. Oils. Rune stones. Mojo bags. Powders. Incense. Artifacts. Human Bone

~~~

Molly nosed around the greenhouse, seemingly expressing a special interest in one spot by the door where she lingered. Then she trotted around to the rear of the potting shed and began snuffling in earnest. Still, no signal.

Dalton was disappointed. She had figured they were standing in a graveyard, but the dog evidently thought otherwise. She looked at the animal, half expecting it any minute now to start rolling in whatever was so appealing back there. Doubts were beginning to surface about this dog's ability, no matter what Tatem had said. Truth is, the poor thing just didn't fit her picture of a cadaver dog. Look at it. Long wavy hair spilling over her eyes like bangs. A tail much too long for her body. Probably would make someone a good pet. Definitely would be more suited to another line of work.

"Think you ought to take her inside the shed?" she asked Tatem.

"Molly," he called, pushing open the door. "In here, girl."

The dog quickly obeyed his command.

"Good dog!" Tatem encouraged. "Find 'em!"

Molly practically shrugged her shoulders once inside and looked back at her handler with a miffed expression.

"Well, it was good idea," Dalton said resignedly. "Jason, let's go back to the house. I want to take the rest of those animal skeletons and have the medical examiner look at them."

The detectives had gotten the house keys from the lawyer handling the estate when they'd delivered a copy of the warrant to him.

"Sorry, we didn't find anything here, detective," Tatem said. "But if there had been a body, Molly would've told us. When she signals, she sits. She never misses."

"I'm sure she doesn't," Dalton replied sweetly, casting a disgusted look toward the dog.

"Tell you what," he said. "I'm going to hook her up and do a spiral search starting from here. If after a few turns we find nothing, then I'll let her range around the grounds on her own a little more."

"Be my guest," Dalton smiled.

The officer put Molly on her leash and, with her nose lowered, they began the circling pattern. Dalton and Rivers started back to the house. She was about to stick the key in the front door lock when she heard Tatem shout from afar.

"Detectives!"

~~~

The desert town of Acton lies hidden in the Sierra Pelota Mountains fifty miles north of downtown Los Angeles. Named by a gold miner in 1887 – who happened to be from Acton, Massachusetts – it was once considered for the state capitol. Things have since slowed down and now it's another bedroom community for the LA commute.

George Overton's house was a low-slung ranch style set back from the road on five acres of parched desert and tumbleweeds. Emilio Zaragoza turned into the driveway's entrance, which was marked by an old wooden wagon, the house number painted on its side.

He parked the Land Rover in front and walked up on the porch. There was no doorbell, so he banged on the screen door. A dog barked madly from inside.

""Be quiet, Henry!" a woman commanded and came to the door. She cradled a yapping Chihuahua in one arm.

"Hi there," Zaragoza smiled. "I'm with the Sheriffs Department."

The woman stared at him blankly with oval yellowish eyes.

"I'd like to speak with George Overton," he continued. "He does live here, I assume?"

"Is this about him running that stop sign?" she asked, sweeping back her hair with the free arm. "We've already paid the ticket."

"No, ma'am, it's about another matter. Are you Mrs. Overton?"

"Another matter?" she repeated anxiously.

"He may have some information about a case I'm investigating."

A trace of fear coursed through her eyes.

"George isn't home," she blurted.

"Perhaps you can help me. May I come in?"

"Better not," she said. "Might upset the dog."

Why is she stonewalling me, Zaragoza wondered? He was beginning to get a strange vibe from this woman. Also, there was something familiar about her but he couldn't place what or where.

"All right," he said, removing a business card from his pocket. "Please have him call me when he gets home. Tell him it's important."

Cass cracked open the screen door wide enough to take his business card. She gave it a cursory look and then slammed the front door shut.

Zaragoza considered knocking again and upping the ante with some direct questions but then thought otherwise. Maybe the woman didn't want to let a stranger in the house. Cop or not. He couldn't blame her. But his gut told him something else was going on. He checked his watch. He'd passed a nice restaurant back in town. An early dinner sounded like the right call while he waited for George Overton to come home.

He got in the Land Rover and drove off.

CHAPTER 17

The Scientific Investigation Division (SID) is responsible for the collection, comparison and interpretation of physical evidence found at crime scenes or collected from suspects and victims. So states the official site of the Los Angeles Police Department.

Dalton had called SID and a field investigation unit was on the way to the Hodges estate. Also, two patrol cars with uniform officers had come to the scene and were standing by to close off the area and keep the traffic moving on Mulholland Drive.

When Tatem had yelled earlier, she and Rivers had raced back to where they'd been searching. Molly had signaled near a clump of Manzanita shrubs. Rather than examine the spot themselves, which could possibly destroy evidence, Dalton opted for the SID experts. She now had a different opinion of the little cadaver dog.

She and Rivers were waiting at the greenhouse with a uniformed officer when his radio buzzed that the techs had arrived.

"Bring them down here," she told the officer.

Four technicians had answered the call. Now the crime scene belonged to them. They would document everything every step of the way.

They began by making a grid of the area. Photographs were taken and measurements made. Next they started to carefully excavate the site where Molly had signaled. It turned out to be a shallow grave.

"Over here, Detectives," one of them called.

Dalton and Rivers approached the patch of ground where the technician was working. The man had brushed away some earth to reveal human skeletal remains, the right scapula and humerus. He continued to remove more of the earth. The body appeared to be facing down.

Suddenly she was startled by a high-pitched whirling sound and looked up. A drone hovered barely twenty feet above them.

"What the hell?" she said in alarm.

"There!" a technician shouted, pointing to a neighboring house. "Guy out on the deck."

Dalton turned to look and saw a neighboring house jutting out from the steep slope and supported by stilts about two and a half blocks away. A large deck stretched across the back where the man was standing. A woman was with him.

"He's holding a box or something in his hands," the tech said, squinting his eyes. "Got to be who's flying the drone."

The small aircraft darted to the side for another angle. Everyone involuntarily ducked.

"Must be taking pictures," the tech suggested.

Anger boiled up in Dalton. She had read in the papers how drones were becoming a hazard to firefighters. She expected it wouldn't be long before one took down a helicopter or even an airliner. She turned to Rivers.

"Get over there, Jason, and tell that dumb shit I'm going to have one of my officers blow his toy out of the air if he doesn't move the damn thing away from here. If he gives you any crap, arrest him for interfering with a police investigation."

Rivers ran back to the house and got hold of a uniformed officer. They jumped in a patrol car and sped away.

Dalton walked over to where she had a better view.

The police car had stopped in front of the house. A moment later she saw Rivers and the officer come out onto the deck followed by a woman. Overhead the drone hovered and drifted. The man appeared to be arguing with the detective. Dalton's phone rang. It was Rivers.

"This guy's being a hard case. Says there's no law against flying his drone anywhere as long as he's below 400 feet. His wife's trying to reason with him but she isn't getting anywhere."

"Arrest him for interfering with an investigation and endangerment," Dalton ordered. "Cuff him so there's no misunderstanding."

She saw Rivers put his hand on the man's arm and turn him around. The drone suddenly spun out of control and flew into the ground close to where Dalton stood and practically scaring the bejesus out of her. It was a spidery-looking gadget.

She picked it up and saw that two of its four rotors had broken in the crash and also that there was a camera fastened to its bottom. She called Rivers, who appeared to now have the man in custody.

"Stop by here and get his fucking model airplane. Mark it for evidence. Then have the officer transport it and him to Van Nuys."

She took a deep breath and returned to the site.

The technician was scraping away more of the earth to expose the skeleton when he made a shocking discovery.

"There's no head," he said, looking up to Dalton.

She bent down to see. The medical examiner's comment flashed through her mind. He had determined that the skull and hands had not been surgically removed. Could they have once belonged to this victim? A chill crept down her spine.

"Are you at a place where you can see the hands?" she asked.

"No, and I can't rush this. In fact, we should stop to document everything at this point. You can never take too many pictures."

He stood and called for the photographer. Dalton walked back to the greenhouse, where she ran into Rivers who had just returned.

"His name is Patrick Drew," Rivers reported. "Apparently, he'd just bought the drone and was trying it out."

"He up in the car?"

"Cuffed and in the back seat. Seems a little upset."

"I'll go talk with him. You stay here."

She grabbed up the drone and carried it with her. The patrol car waited out front with the detainee, who looked out the door window at her approach. He had a glum expression.

"This belong to you?" Dalton asked, opening the door and showing him the drone.

"Yes," he said ruefully.

"Have you any idea of how close this thing was coming to us?"

She shook the drone for emphasis.

"No, I didn't mean to frighten anyone. I thought I was okay. I'm sorry."

"You should be sorry. Suppose you'd hit someone? In fact, your stupid toy almost hit me when it crashed. If I'd been injured, believe me, you would be in a whole lot more trouble than you are now. Do you realize that?"

"I know. It was dumb. I just didn't think."

Dalton stood back from the open door for a moment and sized up the man. Then she reached in and unfastened his seat belt.

"Get out of the car," she told him.

When he was on his feet, she turned him around and removed the handcuffs.

"Erase everything in that camera," she ordered, pointing at the drone.

Drew unclipped the camera fasteners and removed it

to delete the chip.

"Good," Dalton said. "Now, give me that chip."

He meekly complied.

"Did Detective Rivers explain that a police investigation was in progress when he first approached you?" she asked, putting the chip in her pocket.

"Yes, he did."

"So why didn't you bring your drone back right then instead of arguing with him?"

"I didn't believe I was doing anything wrong," he pled. "The place I bought the drone said to just keep it under 400 feet and stay away from airports. I didn't know. I was just curious about what was going on."

"I see," Dalton said, shaking her head in disbelief. Some people, she thought to herself. "Well, for your information, you could go to jail for this. Where do you work?"

"I'm an assistant bank manager. Just got promoted. We were celebrating that today."

Dalton gave him a look.

"Being an assistant bank manager must pay well, "she said, indicating the house. "Expensive house. Expensive toys."

"Oh, my wife's parents own the house," Drew said, almost apologetically. "We couldn't afford anything like that. They've been away visiting relatives back east and should return day after tomorrow. We drop by to check on the house for them."

Dalton nodded.

"How do you think your boss at the bank is going to feel when he learns you're in jail?" she asked.

"I suppose he'll fire me," Drew answered resignedly. "They've been cutting back."

"I wouldn't be surprised if he does," Dalton agreed. "How long have your in-laws lived in that house?"

"Gosh, I don't know. Kamila grew up there."

"That your wife's name, Kamila?" Dalton asked, taking out her phone. "What's the telephone number at the house?"

Drew gave it to her and she called. A worried voice answered.

"This is Detective Laura Dalton with the Los Angeles Police Department. Are you Kamila Drew?"

"Yes, I am," the woman said nervously. "Look, I'm so sorry about this. Pat didn't mean to cause any trouble. Is he at the jail now? I'd like to see if I can get him out. He can't miss work tomorrow."

"Mrs. Drew, your husband is at the house next door where all the police cars are parked out front. Can you come here and pick him up?"

Ironically, a Channel 5 news helicopter whup-whupped into view.

~~~

"You're back," Alison Gordon greeted.

Jack had just come into the bookstore.

"Yeah, I was passing by," he said. "Thought I'd drop in. So you remember me, huh?"

"Of course I remember you. Anyone who's a friend of Aleister Crowley is a friend of mine."

Jack smiled lopsidedly.

"I never could find that guy," he said.

"I told you to go to hell," she laughed. "Did you?"

"Probably will if I don't change my ways. To tell the truth, I came here on purpose. Saw your card posted on a tree at the Rock Store."

He took out the business card from his wallet. Alison looked at him curiously.

"And?" she smiled.

"The card says you carry occult supplies. Maybe you can help me out with something. I found this in the desert."

He removed the folded bill containing the salt and opened it.

"Can you identify this?" he asked.

"Sand?"

"No, it's salt. But I have a feeling that it might have been used for something other than seasoning."

"Let me taste it," she said dabbing with her finger. "Sea salt. It's a little courser than regular table salt. Cooks think it adds more to a dish. People also put it in baths. Believe it does good. And, since you're so interested in the beyond, it's used in occult ceremonies."

"Yeah?"

"So what else did you want to know?" Alison asked.

"Don't suppose you could tell where it came from, could you?"

"Probably the ocean. Where did you say you got it?"

"On a dry lake bed."

"I'm not surprised. Those were once shallow seas."

"Well, this salt was found at the scene of a murder."

~~~

Zaragoza took the last bite of steak and checked his watch. He still had a little time before he should leave. He looked to get the server's attention, a middle-aged woman with red permed hair named Wanda. She spotted him and came over.

"What can I get you, sugar?"

"Just a refill," he said, indicating his coffee cup.

"How was your steak?" she asked, topping up with the pot she'd brought over.

He had ordered the New York strip done medium rare with a side of sliced tomatoes instead of the stuffed baked potato.

"Think it was the best I've ever eaten," he said. "Really."

Wanda smiled coyly.

"Well, we do pride ourselves on our steaks. All of our beef is grass-fed and come from the same ranch. Can I get you some dessert. Got a peach pie just out of the oven."

"Oh, that's temping," Zaragoza grinned. "But I better not. Belt is getting a little tight."

"Skinny thing like you?" Wanda joked. "Come on, now. I'll even put a scoop of ice cream on it."

Zaragoza resisted the offer, paid the bill and left a nice tip. On the way to the Overtons, he went over some questions he intended to ask. He'd been flying blind up until Brian Gordon mentioned that he lived in West Hollywood. That, coupled with what his deputy had told him about the domestic violence report involving a person with the same name as Gordon's cameraman, had intrigued him. Was it the same guy? He had run the name and had gotten no hits. That didn't mean there wasn't a history of violence. He just hadn't been arrested.

~~~

Alison Gordon took a long drag on the cigarette, blew the smoke out and apologized.

"I hope the smoke doesn't bother you," she said. "I'd stopped smoking. But you know how it is."

"It's fine," Jack told her. "Don't worry about it. I've quit many times myself."

She'd stepped out on the sidewalk and Jack had followed.

"It's just when, well, you said that your friend had been murdered and all, I just ... I don't know, for some reason it hit me hard."

Jack reached his arms around her and gave a hug.

"Did the police tell you how it happened?" she asked.

"No details," he said, dropping his arms and letting her go. "Only that he'd been found in a burned-out car on the dry lake."

"And the salt was spread around the car, you said? Like in a circle?"

"That's right."

Alison considered that.

"Salt's often used in rituals. Not always bad but sometimes."

"Would our mutual friend, Aleister Crowley, have used it in one of his little parties?"

"You wouldn't want to have been invited."

"Look, here's something else you ought to know."

Jack then filled her in on the human skull and everything that had happened at the Hodges estate. When he'd finished, Alison looked at him with a frightened expression in her eyes.

"Jack, you need to be very careful," she warned. "I don't know who is involved, but if what is going on is what I think it is, you are in extreme danger."

"I'm not sure I believe in evil spirits," he said. "Just that there are evil people."

Jack had indeed experienced true evil.

"This is going to sound silly," Alison said with a little laugh. "My brother and his wife are giving a small dinner party tonight. They live in West Hollywood. Would you be my date?"

~~~

The Land Rover eased slowly down the driveway and parked next to a double-cab pickup truck. It was early evening and the sun had dropped below the western mountains, leaving the urbanized desert in subdued light.

Zaragoza knocked on the front door. He could hear the television playing from inside. Channel 5 news. He knocked again, louder. A dog began yapping.

"I'm coming!" a man's voice called out. "Hold your damn horses."

This was to be an interview, he reminded himself. Not

an interrogation. Whether Overton would openly talk was up for grabs. He could be asked to leave at any time. One tactic he liked was to build a line of questions designed to make the person being interviewed lie. Then you had him.

The volume on the TV set lowered and a moment later the door opened. A medium- sized man wearing a western shirt and jeans stood there in his stocking feet. A tiny dog danced around him growling ferociously.

"Mr. Overton? I'm Emilio Zaragoza with the Los Angeles Sheriffs."

"Hang on a second," Overton said, then yelled over his shoulder. "Cass, come and get Henry, will you?"

The woman Zaragoza had earlier spoken with appeared and swept up the grumbling Henry.

"He's a good watchdog," Overton said. "Gets a little anxious sometimes, though. What can I do for you, Sheriff?"

"I'm investigating a homicide that took place on a dry lakebed not to far from here. I understand you were filming a commercial out there."

"Yeah, I heard about that thing," Overton said. "Kind of scary, person getting killed right where we'd been. You know who it was?"

"We're working on the identification," Zaragoza said. "May I come in?"

"Sure," Overton shrugged. "Cass, put the dog in the damn kitchen."

"Good evening, Mrs. Overton," Zaragoza nodded, stepping through the door.

"Cass told me you'd dropped by earlier today," George said. "Don't know how much I can help with your investigation. Sure wasn't any murder going on when we were there. Let's go in the den. Be more comfortable."

The den was ordinary. Pine-paneled walls. No photographs, pictures or anything of a personal nature lying around. Fake fireplace with an electric heater. Bookcase partially filled with nondescript volumes. Brown vinyl sofa and two matching chairs. George offered one to Zaragoza. He and Cass sat on the sofa.

"Titan Films gave us the crew list," Zaragoza began. "I'm just running through it."

"Yeah? They should've told us that the cops were coming," Overton said in an annoyed tone. "I'm not sure I should say anything."

"That's entirely up to you, Mr. Overton. This is just routine, but if you don't feel comfortable, I can leave."

Cass nodded as if to say she'd be fine with the detective leaving.

"Brian Gordon said that you were the director as well as the cameraman," Zaragoza smiled. "That's a pretty big responsibility, I'd imagine, wearing two hats. How do you keep everything together?"

Overton relaxed.

"The cameraman's central," he grinned. "Everybody makes a big deal over the director but half the time he doesn't do shit. Like they say, behind every bullhorn stands a hack. I've done this work for so long I don't even have to think about it."

"Well, you could've fooled me," Zaragoza laughed. "All those people running around doing this and doing that. I'd be lost, myself."

"Hell, the secret is getting good people. Everybody knows his job. All I have to do then is yell 'action' and 'cut'. It's not rocket science, man. A good eye helps, though."

"Ah, so it's the crew that's important," Zaragoza said. "Is yours always the same?"

"Most times. Occasionally, you have to fill in with somebody else."

"What about the day you were filming at the dry lake?" Zaragoza asked. "Same crew?"

"Sure. Why does that matter to you?"

"Just want to make sure there were no strangers. Someone perhaps looking around. Had no business being there."

"You mean, like casing the joint?" Overton guffawed. "Well, the client came out for awhile. And Brian Gordon."

"Right, but what I'm getting at is you didn't see anyone unusual. By that I mean, spectators or such."

Overton laughed again.

"Man, we were in the desert. It was a hundred fucking degrees. Not too many people out for a stroll."

Zaragoza chuckled.

"I guess you would have to know where you were going or else you might get lost," he said. "Do you use that location often?"

"Must've shot ten or twelve commercials at that same spot. A lot of production companies use that dry lake."

"Say, you two remind me of a couple I may have met," Zaragoza said offhandedly.

Jack Hunter's description of the two uninvited visitors had popped up in his mind as soon as he'd walked in the house. Lanky guy with iron-gray hair. Cat-eyed woman with long black hair. He decided to pursue it.

"Can't remember where," he continued. "Maybe Malibu? You guys ever go out there? It's on my beat every now and then."

"Long way from here," Overton said, shaking his head. "Not any reason to make the trek. Don't think I've been to Malibu in, hell, at least a year. Maybe longer."

Cass shifted uneasily in her seat.

"I should go check on Henry," she said to George.

"Think I know," Zaragoza said, holding up his finger. "Was it West Hollywood? I worked there a few years back."

"Don't believe it was West Hollywood," Overton said

with a smarmy smile. "I'm not of that persuasion, if you catch my drift."

"Not important," Zaragoza told him. "I run into so many people in my line of work, pretty soon I start mixing them up."

"Anything more I can help you with, Sheriff?"

"No, sir, thank you and Mrs. Overton for your time."

CHAPTER 18

In a homicide investigation, the detective also becomes a victim. You are a witness of other people's trauma. No cop has ever said it doesn't get to him. Sometimes gallows humor helped. Other times nothing did.

One of Dalton's defenses was to busy herself at the crime scene. As lead detective she was responsible for making sure nothing was left undone. There were layers of information to be gathered. A crime scene log to be kept. An inventory taken. Documentation with photographs, video, measurements, even sketches made, if necessary. And through every step to always ensure contamination control.

The team was about ready to wrap up for the day. SID had removed the skeletal corpse from its makeshift grave. They'd found no skull. Also, they had discovered the hands were missing. Countless pictures had been taken. The remains were carefully bagged and taken to the county morgue. Dalton had ordered the animal skeletons inside the house to be taken there for examination as well.

Molly, the cadaver dog, had sniffed the entire estate but had come up empty. Still, Dalton planned on doing another search for any possible evidence. No dog, just cops, providing she could scrounge the manpower. Otherwise, she and Rivers would beat the bushes themselves.

Yellow crime scene tape had been strung anew on the property fence running along Mulholland. Patrol would keep an eye on everything.

Shadows stretched their full length eastward to announce the day was nearing its end. Dalton was ready for a long hot shower and a large glass of wine. But there was a report to write. She got into the Porsche and drove to Coldwater Canyon and down to the station in Van Nuys. She felt beat to hell.

Tom Bradshaw had left by the time she arrived. He'd gone home early to get ready for a retirement party later that night. A detective III in Hollywood was pulling the pin after thirty years with the Department. Bradshaw had partnered with the man when they'd both worked patrol.

She placed her briefcase on the table and began pulling out the crime scene documents. Notes, general observations, anything and everything, all of which would be entered in the murder book.

Every homicide had its own murder book. It was a physical book in which every scrap of evidence was listed as it became available, as well as a step-by-step log of the detective's progress in the investigation which would hopefully end with the crime being solved. As such, it became a witness to a murder.

Rivers came into the detectives room with a bag of McDonalds.

"Cheeseburgers okay?" he asked. "Got fries, too."

Of course you do, Dalton thought, and smiled.

"Great, Jason. Just updating the murder book."

"What a day!" Rivers said, taking a burger and order of fries out of the bag. "Then that asshole with the drone. Why'd you let him go?"

"One more hassle we don't need right now," Dalton told him, fingering some of the fries. "Press would've made a big deal out of it. Poor guy might've lost his job, too. Anyway, I think he got the point. No need for overkill."

Rivers tore open a ketchup pack and squeezed it out on the fries.

"I don't know," he said. "I would've hauled his ass in."

"Yeah, well, maybe you're right. Let's talk about this case."

Rivers scooted his chair closer.

"There's no question in my mind that the body is Alvis Hume," Dalton began. "Skull missing. Hands missing. It'd be the biggest coincidence ever if it isn't. You agree?"

Rivers nodded.

"So going with that assumption, here's what I want you to do next."

Rivers took out a pen and small notebook.

"Find out everything you can about Hume. Where he was from, friends, last address before prison, work, criminal record, all that good stuff. And then check with Corcoran. What was he like there during his incarceration. Good boy? Bad boy? Keep to himself? Any gang affiliations? What was his prison job? Also, his cellmates. Was he a good cellie? Get their names and run down their records. Are any of them still inside?"

"This is going to be a long phone call," Rivers said after he'd finished writing.

"Drive up there if you have to," Dalton said.

"Why the focus on Corcoran?" Rivers asked.

"It might tell why he lost his head."

Later, Francine phoned with a rundown on the Weird Dave Show. Turns out the Hodges estate has now become a body farm, according to Dave.

~~~

Zaragoza had driven back to his office from Acton. Business was slow and only a few officers were on duty. Grabbing a cup of coffee, he went to his desk and called Deputy Charles Brinkley.

"Hope I'm not interrupting your dinner," he said. "Just finished talking with George Overton and want to run a couple of ideas past you."

"Not interrupting at all," Brinkley told him. "Fire ahead."

Zaragoza had written down some notes about the

conversation as soon as he'd left the house. First and foremost, the guy was lying.

"About that log you kept when you worked West Hollywood," Zaragoza began. "Did you follow up on that domestic?"

"Actually, I did. Went back a week later. Talked with the wife. She was very cool. Swore everything was fine. Is this Overton the same guy?"

"I believe so. Here's the thing."

Zaragoza went over the entire interview with his deputy. Including Overton's denial of having lived in West Hollywood and his insistence of not having been in Malibu, despite the pair of them perfectly matching Jack Hunter's description.

"The woman was nervous," he continued. "First time when I came to the house and then again during the interview. Something's going on with her."

"The lady who called in the domestic was a neighbor. Ginger Ballard. Got her address and telephone number if you want it."

What an amazing piece of luck, Zaragoza thought.

"Yeah, I want it. Wonder if she still lives there?"

"As I recall, she was in her thirties," Brinkley went on. "Nice person. Attractive. Her house was next door. She and her husband lived there. Believe they were the owners. Said it wasn't the first time there'd been trouble at their neighbors."

Fucking guy must have the memory of an elephant, Zaragoza said to himself.

"All right, Charles, I'm going to call her but could be the numbers been changed or dropped. Everyone uses a cell now."

Zaragoza rang off with his deputy and punched in the telephone number for Ginger Ballard. She picked up on the second ring. He identified himself and told her that he was trying to locate a former neighbor, Beth Overton.

"My God, has something finally happened to that poor woman?" Ginger asked anxiously.

"Not to my knowledge. Do you have any reason to believe so?"

"She was married to a real bastard. I worried that he might kill her."

"You're talking about George Overton, I presume," Zaragoza said, taking a chance.

"I'm talking about the goddamn devil!"

"Ma'am, I'd like to come by and show you a picture of George Overton and you can tell me if he's the same person I'm talking about. What would be a convenient time?"

"Tomorrow morning's okay. You have my address?"

Zaragoza wrote it down, though it was the same that Brinkley had given him, and said he'd be there at nine.

CHAPTER 19

By a miracle, Jack found a parking space two blocks over, in Beverly Hills. Make that a double miracle since it had no time restriction as far as he could tell. He felt guilty about taking it. There had to be a catch.

The Gordons' apartment was on North Doheny Drive in a new high-rise. It was still light and a pleasant walk. He fastened the radio cover plate in place and switched off the battery kill which was hidden beneath the driver's seat. There were no side curtains on the Jeep. Anyone trying to futz around inside would be exposed. They do steal things even in Beverly Hills. He set off for Doheny.

Alison had suggested they go in separate cars. That way, if Jack got bored, he could leave. Which, in Jack's mind, was very likely to happen. When he'd asked, she'd said it was to be just a casual gathering, so he had dressed accordingly in a black blazer, designer jeans and a fitted cotton shirt in dark green. He wore the collar open.

Jack introduced himself to the doorman and was told the Gordons lived on the twenty-second floor. The elevator silently whooshed him upward to a gentle stop and opened to reveal a vestibule with four apartments. The door of one was ajar and a murmur of conversation spilled out from within. Jack pushed the bell. A striking-looking blonde swept back the door. Her body said 'made in Beverly Hills'.

"I'm Jack Hunter. Alison invited me. Are you Mrs. Gordon?"

"Heavens no, darling." she cooed. "But please do come in."

There were forty people or so milling around the large living room. All dressed to the nines. Some stood in little groups. Jack pegged them for industry types. A guy noodled on a baby grand piano in one corner. French doors opened onto a balcony with a sweeping view of the Pacific Ocean.

"Get you a drink, sir?" a man dressed in a short white jacket asked.

"Sparkling water, please. Oh, and with a lime."

The man disappeared and Jack continued to take in the room. It was quite a place. A large Hockney painting commanded one wall. Furniture, from what he could tell, looked Italian and expensive.

"Just make yourself at home, darling," the blonde said, offering a smile that'd be cast in a minute for a tooth whitener ad. "There are munchies on the side table, yum, yum," she added before leaving him standing.

The man returned with his drink and Jack began to move around the room. He didn't recognize a single face. Once you're out of the business, you're out, period. And he'd been out for some time.

"Jack!" a woman called.

He turned to see Alison wave. She was on the balcony with a couple of men. She had on a little black thing. The guys wore tuxes.

"Come with me," she said, rushing over and taking his hand. She led him back to the balcony.

"Brian, I'd like you to meet Jack Hunter." And then, "Jack, this is my brother, Brian Gordon."

There was no denying that. He possessed an amazing resemblance to his sister. High cheekbones and a strong mouth. And both were equally tall.

"Pleasure to meet you, Jack," he smiled genuinely, offering his hand. "And this is my wife, Dag Dahlmgardt."

Dag was not quite as tall as Brian. He had curly red hair and blue eyes that expressed kindness. He seemed to be physically fit but not overly muscled. The advantage of having a good trainer. He stuck out his hand.

"Nice to meet you, Jack. So you're a friend of Alison?"

"Not a close friend," Jack said. "But we share some mutual interests."

Brian raised his eyebrows.

"How's that?" he asked.

"I'm doing research on the occult," Jack told him. "She's helping me."

"Well, you're lucky," Brian said. "Alison knows her stuff when it comes to the mysterious. Where did you first meet?"

"In her bookshop."

"Are you writing a book?" Dag asked curiously, adding a little laugh. "I mean, are you a famous author? Should I know you?"

"No, this is a hobby. Something I've recently taken up."

"Jack manages real estate," Alison said.

"Not a bad business to be in these days," Brian commented. "You always done that, Jack?"

"Fell into it. I used to work in advertising. I was a producer at an agency."

Brian took notice of this.

"Here in town?"

"Gaysome Hough. You know them?"

"Best agency in LA. They do great work. Why'd you get out of the business?"

"Matter of principle."

Brian paused for a moment.

"Ever consider coming back?" he asked. "I own a production company. Titan Films."

"Yeah, I've heard of Titan," Jack said. "Never had a chance to work with you."

Brian smiled.

"Truth is, I'm looking for a line producer. I have this really terrific director who's also a great cameraman. Right now, he's with us on a freelance basis. I want to make him staff. Team him up with a good producer. Maybe someone like yourself."

"I don't know," Jack said hesitantly. "It's been awhile and I've got my own thing going. What's your guy's name?"

"George Overton. He's a real sweetheart. Tell you what. We're doing a spot for your old agency tomorrow. Fashion shoot for a change. Should be fun. Why don't you drop by the location. Say hello to George, okay? Tell him we talked."

Jack didn't know quite what to say. He really wasn't interested in meeting the cameraman but the idea of hanging out at a shoot appealed. It had been a long while.

"So where's the location?"

"Santa Monica Pier."

"Come on, Jack," Alison said, taking him by the arm. "I'll introduce you to some people."

They walked over to the buffet.

"Hungry?" Alison asked, picking up a shrimp. "These are delicious."

"No, thanks."

He looked around the room listening to the buzz, twitters of laughter. Some checking out others. Others posturing to be checked out. This was no longer his crowd, he realized. His mind once again sped a couple of thousand miles to the other side of the country and down to Key West. To the eclectic and eccentric group of characters he knew there. A whole different league and one he definitely preferred. Nostalgia overwhelmed him. He ought to leave this scene right now but that wouldn't be fair to Alison.

"I was just thinking about Dan Tana's," she whispered in his ear.

"Why don't we blow this joint then," he said.

The popular restaurant was only a few blocks away on Santa Monica Boulevard. They took Alison's BMW, which had been parked in the building's basement. A small line waited outside by the door. Alison said something to the maître' d and they were immediately shown to a tiny table in the corner.

"Come here often?" Jack grinned, once they were seated.

"He knows my brother."

"Good to know people in high places. I used to eat here when I worked at the agency. But now, I don't know, just don't get around much any more."

"Sounds like an old song," Alison laughed.

The waiter came and they ordered a glass of wine. Jack noticed several appreciative glances being given to Alison by the men a couple of tables over. He didn't blame them.

"Jack, this is kind of awkward but my brother's job offer might not be in your best interest."

"You've lost me," Jack said. "Why?"

Alison frowned.

"It has nothing to do with Brian. It's that story you told me about the human skull in the car you bought from the Hodges estate. Brian knew Martin Hodges."

"Jesus, what are you saying?"

Alison took a sip of her wine.

"Both Brian and Martin were crazy about Porsches. But Martin wasn't a very nice person. And neither were some of his friends. George Overton was one."

Jack was silent for a moment.

"How do you know all this?" he asked finally.

"Brian once took me to Martin's house. There was a party. I couldn't stand the people. They were scary. He'd warned me that Martin dabbled in the occult. Joked about the dark side. Things started getting out of hand. I finally called a taxi and left."

"Do you think your brother is involved with the skull?"

"No, Brian's simply nuts about cars."

Jack considered everything she'd just told him and also what he'd learned and experienced so far. The use of salt in rituals. The skull in a box. Hodges estate. Mike Eaton's horrible death. Prowlers at his house. Uninvited visitors. The Jaguar. Topanga. Xanadu. Alison, herself?

He felt they were all somehow connected. But where to begin to get them all together?

The waiter stopped at the table but Jack waved him away.

"I have a friend with the LAPD," he said. "She's the detective who's investigating the shooting at the Hodges. I'd like to tell her about that party if that's okay with you."

"Guess so. But I don't want Brian's name brought into it. "

"That's fine with me."

"Actually, Brian met Dag through Martin. They'd once collaborated on a short film."

"I must've missed it," Jack joked.

Alison sighed.

"Jack, I like you very much and really want to see you again. But if you don't mind, right now I need to go home. Okay?"

"Sure."

Jack left a hundred dollar bill on the table. Alison drove him to where he'd parked. She leaned over and kissed him hard on the lips and then left without saying a word. He stood watching as her taillights disappeared at the next corner and then he got into the Jeep. He decided to take a ride down Sunset Strip while it was still there. Plans were already in the works to turn the famous landmark into another canyon of high-rise hotels.

CHAPTER 20

Ginger Ballard lived in a small bungalow on a side street south of Melrose Avenue. It was a white-stuccoed structure with a terra cotta tiled roof, one of a million lookalikes in LA.

Zaragoza parked at the curb in front of the house. He got out and looked up and down the street. Not one other soul stirred. Well, it was nine o'clock in the morning. What the hell did he expect, a parade? He smiled to himself and rang the doorbell.

A woman appearing to be in her late thirties answered. She could've actually been in her early fifties, for all he knew. This *was* Hollywood. She had on beige slacks and a dark brown fitted blouse which showed off a nice figure. A pretty face blessed with a few freckles and hazel eyes. Her auburn hair cut to shoulder length.

"Mrs. Ballard? I'm Emilio Zaragoza."

"Ginger will be fine."

She led him into the living room. It was decorated in southwestern style with a couple of brightly colored scatter rugs spread on the dark wooden floor. A nice painting by Bert Geer Phillips of the Taos School hung on one wall.

"Have a seat," she said. "Would you like a cup of coffee?"

Zaragoza told her that he would and thanked her for offering. A moment later she was back with a tray containing a small pot and two cups.

"Help yourself to cream and sugar," she said, pouring his cup.

Zaragoza added a touch of cream.

"Good coffee," he said after a sip.

"It's French. I get it at the Farmer's Market."

"I'll have to stop there on the way home. What do you do, Miss Ballard?"

"I work at Paramount. I'm Pauline Gretes' assistant. She's a producer."

Then Ginger got down to business.

"Now, you wanted to know about George Overton," she said matter-of-factly. "He's a motherfucker who ought to be in prison."

Zaragoza was momentarily startled by her virulence.

"Perhaps so," he said, "but first, I'd like to show you a photograph to make sure we're talking about the same person."

He took out a photo of Overton he'd gotten from the DMV and gave it to her.

"That's the motherfucker," Ginger said bitterly.

"When did you first meet the Overtons?" Zaragoza asked.

"They moved into the house next door ... when was it? Time gets away from me."

"Do you know where they'd lived before?"

"Not really. Beth had some family back east. Florida, I believe she said, but I don't think that's where they moved here from. George might've been from Arizona. Don't know for sure. He was a cameraman so I imagine they've been in this area for a while."

"And what was she like? Beth, that is."

"Aren't you supposed to be taking notes or something?" Ginger asked.

Zaragoza laughed.

"It's okay. I have a good memory. Besides writing down things is distracting."

"If you say so. Where was I? Oh, yeah, Beth. Nicest person you'd ever want to meet. Christian lady. Not that I'm much of a churchgoer myself."

"Sounds like a good neighbor," Zaragoza said. "What

happened?"

"George fucking Overton happened. They'd been here about a month when they started having these terrible arguments. Always ended with Beth crying."

"What about physical violence?"

"I never saw any but the fights got worse. I finally had to call the police."

"And how about your husband? Did he ever witness any violence between them?"

Ginger gave a small bitter laugh.

"Mark wouldn't have said anything even if he had. See no evil, etcetera, etcetera was his motto."

Zaragoza wondered if the husband *had* seen more and just didn't want to become involved. Wouldn't be the first time.

"Perhaps I should also talk with him," he suggested.

"Be my guest," Ginger said. "I think he's living in Phoenix, Arizona. We were divorced last year. Yeah, I got the house."

"Well, maybe that won't be necessary. You said the fights got worse. What did you mean actually by worse? Noisier? Longer?"

Ginger considered.

"I mean, he wasn't exactly beating her but he was still hurting her, you know?"

Zaragoza didn't reply but waited for her to explain.

"Kinky sex. At least that's what I thought."

"That's not a crime," Zaragoza said.

"Believe me, this was a crime," Ginger insisted. "He wasn't making love. He was just fucking her. Oral. Anal. You name it, he poked it. Got his rocks off by hurting her. She begged him not to. But he didn't care. Said it was her duty to serve him."

"And she told you that?"

"I was the only person she could talk to. I suggested

she go to a marriage counselor. Then it got even worse. He started raping her."

"Did she report it?"

"Are you kidding?" Ginger scoffed. "She was scared shitless of him."

Ginger looked away momentarily to collect herself.

"Next thing you know, Spencer was dead."

This really caught Zaragoza's attention.

"George started having friends over to party. More of an orgy, really. That's when it happened. Bastard cut the little thing's head off."

Zaragoza took in a deep breath. A child, he thought?

"Who was Spencer?"

"Her cat! He did it right in front of her, too. All those other assholes there thought it was wonderful. Even cheered. Can you imagine something as cruel as that?"

Zaragoza sat back in his chair.

"Beth couldn't take it any longer," Ginger continued. "She came over the next morning and told me she was leaving. She was gone before George got home."

"Did she say where she was going?"

"Just back east. Maybe Florida again. I didn't want to know where."

"What about George?" Zaragoza asked. "Was he upset about her leaving?"

"Not so you'd have known it," Ginger answered disgustedly. "Business as usual for that son of a bitch."

"Did you have any further contact with him?"

"I wouldn't give him the time of day. Tell you what I did do, however. I went out and bought myself a shotgun."

"Was there a reason for that? I mean, did he threaten you?"

"I made sure he knew better than to try. One morning as he was leaving the house, I took my gun outside to the sidewalk so he could see it. Didn't say anything, just smiled at him and came back inside."

"That might have been considered brandishing, Miss Ballard."

"Think so? I considered it reaching an understanding. He moved out not long afterwards."

Zaragoza thanked her for her time and left for his office. He didn't bother stopping at the Farmer's Market.

~~~

Jack climbed out of the Pacific Ocean shivering. The water was freezing. That's often a big surprise to visitors. They figure it must be like Hawaii until they hit the Malibu surf. But a cold swim was what Jack had needed. He walked across the sandy beach back to his house.

He put on the coffeemaker, took a quick hot shower and dressed in a pair of shorts and a sweatshirt with cut-off sleeves. The air was still a little cool. Out on the deck, he got down to the first order of business.

"Homicide, this is Detective Jason Rivers."

Jack had made several attempts to reach Dalton's personal cell and each time it'd gone to message. He'd next called Van Nuys and was transferred to detectives.

"Detective Rivers, Jack Hunter here. Sorry to bother you. Is Detective Dalton free?"

"She's out. Can I help you?"

"No, I'll try later. Tell her I called. Thanks."

He checked his watch. It was mid-morning. Rotten luck that he'd not been able to reach Laura. He believed she'd be interested in what he had learned at the party and his take on what it all meant. He also believed Alison Gordon might know more than she was admitting. Whatever that 'more' might be, he wasn't sure. One thing, though, despite her warning about George Overton, he was going to that commercial filming. He got out of his chair and went inside.

Traffic was light on the PCH at this time of morning.

He took the off-ramp to Santa Monica and drove to his old office building. Street parking had never been good and lately had become impossible. He pulled into the underground garage and got a ticket from the machine. The first level was full. On the second level some jerk had straddled the last two visitor spaces with his Ferrari. He continued on down to the next level reserved for the advertising agency and grabbed a vacant client space.

There wasn't much of a crowd gathered at the foot of the Santa Monica pier. A couple of equipment trucks parked nearby. A trailer, probably for the talent. Light stands and reflectors stationed on the sidewalk. People milling around. He headed for a small group standing by a table laden with snacks and a coffee urn. He figured them for the creative team.

"Hi, guys," he greeted.

Two women, both blondes with close-cropped hair and somewhere in their twenties were engaged in a serious conversation with each other and paid him no attention. A man, also ignored by the women, looked up as Jack approached.

"This the Titan Films shoot?" Jack asked.

"Yeah," the man answered. "Who're you?"

"I'm a friend of Brian's."

"Who?"

"Brian Gordon. He owns Titan."

"Oh, thought you might be a cop checking on our permit. I work for the agency. I'm the writer on this disaster."

The two women had taken their conversation, which had now become heated, to a spot further away.

"That's the art director and producer," the man told him. "They want to kill each other."

Jack laughed.

"Who's the client?" he asked.

"Blue Boy Jeans. But they never send anyone on shoots. Too cheap."

"Where's the director?" he asked. "I was supposed to meet him."

"He's the asshole on the crane over there," the man told him. "He likes you to think he's a great guy but he's an asshole."

Jack looked to where he was pointing. The crane arm boomed up with a man in its bucket shouting directions through a bullhorn. He immediately recognized him.

CHAPTER 21

Alvis Hume's heavily decomposed body rested on the stainless steel examination table in the autopsy suite at the county morgue. A body block, which was a rubber brick, had been positioned beneath the shoulders to thrust the chest forward and make it easier to open. His skull and hands were placed on a smaller table. And on another stood the animal skeletons taken from the Hodges estate in different stages of disarticulation. The scene was almost too much for Dalton to take in.

"I can tell you in all certainty that Mr. Hume was dead before his decapitation," John Logan stated. "Look at this."

The medical examiner pointed to space between two exposed ribs on the body.

"See those marks?" he continued. "He was stabbed right there. My guess would be with a double-edged knife since both ribs are deeply cut. Also, the bone chipping indicates the blade was twisted. Might've penetrated the heart. Certainly made a mess of the lung. I'm going to photograph this area. Could be a signature wound."

"How can you tell about the heart?" Dalton asked and immediately realized it was a dumb question that had nothing to do with anything.

"Decomposition would preclude an answer either way. But I have an interesting speculation for you to consider. More than one person was involved in Mr. Hume's unfortunate condition."

"That went over my head," Dalton said.

"I love your sense of morbid humor, detective," Logan chuckled. "I suspect our murderer didn't separate our victim from his head and hands. In fact, I'd bet on it. Let me show you the skull."

Logan lifted the skull from the table and turned it bottom side up.

"Whoever removed this wasn't a skilled surgeon but did possess a half-decent technique. He used the wrong procedure, of course, but still was somewhat proficient. A better understanding of human anatomy would've helped. But notice that scratch there, see it? Bone chipping, too. Surgeon wouldn't have been that careless."

He next picked up one of the skeletal hands.

"Same thing here. Got a little rough around the carpals. Now let's go back and look at the knife wound. By the way, there was another stab."

Dalton took in a breath. This was more than macabre. It was the stuff madness was made from.

"Here," Logan said, again pointing at the damaged ribs. "You're looking at a forceful and merciless attack. The knife was twisted during the stabbing. Multiple times. The fellow was out to kill with a prejudice, no doubt about it. And here, below the breastbone is that other wound."

He ran his gloved finger along the exposed bone. It revealed a cut mark.

"You mentioned the heart," he said. "That one would've done the trick. But it was unnecessary. He was already dead."

Dalton pictured the assault in her mind. Not pretty.

"Do you think this could have happened during a fight?" she asked.

"Possibly, but in my opinion it was a murder, pure and simple. The victim was grabbed, perhaps even held, while his assailant went to work. In a fight, there would've been defensive wounds. Because the bone damage was on the ribs, I would have expected to see cut marks on the hands and arms. Motive? A forensic psychiatrist might have an opinion or two on the subject. I'd start with hate. That's always a good motive."

"I still don't understand why you believe there were two people involved," Dalton said.

"Couple of things," Logan smiled. "Mr. Hume was brutally attacked to get the job done. We agree the stab wounds confirm that. Now, consider the skull and the hands. They were harvested, if you will, after the fact. How long afterwards, I can't say. But a more delicate touch was used in that instance, indicating a different 'surgeon'. Then, there's one more irrefutable fact."

Logan motioned with his finger for Dalton to follow him. He walked over to the animal skeletons.

"These skeletons weren't professionally prepared," he said. "Probably done by an amateur or a student. However, each shows signs of improving skill. Take the cat."

Dalton looked at the small structure of bones. She didn't like what she saw.

"That one is the oldest," Logan said. "Lots of ham-handed mistakes. Learner's errors. But as you move along and finally come to the goat, you see a better technique. Still some sloppy disarticulation, but better."

He walked back and picked up the human skull.

"And *here* things get even better," he said, offering the bony globe to Dalton, who blanched and declined. "Remember the scratch I showed you before?"

He turned over the skull to show the bottom of the cranium. Dalton peered to see where he was pointing.

"Right here, that slight gouge where C1 would've attached. Apparently, a troublesome spot for our anatomist. You see, each mark made on the bones is like a fingerprint. In this case, it tells me that all of this is the handiwork of one individual, the harvester. And that person is not the one who murdered Mr. Hume."

Dalton pursed her lips, a slight frown wrinkling her brow.

"You seem to have some doubt, detective," Logan

grinned.

"I'll run it by my boss," she finally smiled.

"Oh, I forgot the clincher," Logan said, slapping his hand dramatically to his forehead. "Mr. Hume's assailant was right-handed based on where he'd been stabbed. The direction and depth of the knife marks on the skull tell me they were made by a left-handed person."

<center>~~~</center>

The Sheriffs Department wasn't making much headway on the Eaton murder investigation. Detective Emilio Zaragoza had even considered revisiting the crime scene. He'd decided against it. There was nothing more to be found. Just the end of a road that so far had led to nowhere.

He let his feet fall from the desktop where he'd propped them. Deputy Brinkley, who was in the office with him, glanced over from the report he'd been reading.

"Goddammit, Charles, what's the holdup on Arizona's DMV?" Zaragoza growled. "Did the guy live there or not?"

"Seems there's a problem with their computers," Brinkley said. "Might've been hacked. They'll have to get back to us."

Zaragoza snorted in disgust.

"Of course they've been hacked," he said sarcastically. "Everybody's doing it. Russians, Chinese, Mrs. Smith's eighth-grade class."

Zaragoza's office telephone rang. Brinkley picked up for him.

"Hold on," he said after a moment. It's your best friend, Jack Hunter."

Zaragoza listened silently while Jack talked.

"Let's go back to the beginning," Zaragoza said when Jack had finished. "You went to the dry lake? That's a crime scene. It was marked off."

"Not where I went in," Jack fudged. "It's a mess out

148

there, by the way. Must've been fifty car tracks. Not to mention a ton of litter. Did you notice the salt?"

Zaragoza admitted that he had.

"Right," Jack said excitedly. "Salt's used in rituals. I found that out at the book store in Topanga. Xanadu. Remember? Might be worth checking out. Now, what are you going to do about George Overton?"

Zaragoza sighed.

"Mr. Hunter, I appreciate your help and as far as George Overton goes, his coming into your house wasn't a crime. About the salt you mentioned, yes, I am aware that it's used in certain rituals. And once again, I advise you to stay out of the crime scene."

Jack was flummoxed. There was nothing left to do but thank the detective for his time and hang up.

Zaragoza felt exasperated as he placed the phone into its cradle. All he had were suspicions, no real evidence. He was certain that George Overton was worth keeping a watch on. He thought about the salt Hunter had mentioned. Yeah, it was curious. And it might be worth taking another trip out to the desert after all.

~~~

"Ain't science grand?" Bradshaw chortled. "Truly fucking amazing."

Dalton had finished reporting the Medical Examiner's discovery to her Detective III. They sat at the homicide table in Van Nuys.

"Right-handed killer. Left-handed bone carver. You've got to hand it to ol' John Logan." He laughed heartily at his bon mot. Dalton merely smiled.

"Rivers is on his way to Corcoran," she said. "We decided it would be more productive to talk with them in person."

"It's a nice drive," Bradshaw nodded.

"I think he took his motorcycle."

"Jesus," Bradshaw said. "Must have a death wish. What's he hoping to find by being there that he couldn't learn over the phone?"

"Just face-to-face always seems better," Dalton told him. "Don't you agree? Besides, something inspiring might come up."

"Uh-huh, by the way, did you check back with Hume's parole officer? I know we got his family address from him and the court. But I mean the follow-up on how Hume handled his parole. Remember our talking about that?"

Dalton hesitated.

"I ... no, boss, Guess it just slipped my mind. Jesus! How dumb is that?"

"You said it, I didn't. Give 'em a call. Unless you feel it would be better to talk to them in person."

~~~

Alison Gordon was busy putting up a new shipment of bestsellers for display when Herb Thacker came into the store. He went straight to the section on the occult, sweeping past her without a word.

"See anything you like back there, feel free to help yourself," Alison called after him.

Herb ignored her sarcasm and picked out nine black candles from the case – nine was an evil number – and carried them to the register. Then he returned for three boxes of sea salt – three was an evil number – and brought them up. He slapped down a fifty-dollar bill on the counter.

Alison walked over to the counter, bagged his purchases and gave him his change. Herb left as wordlessly as he'd come.

Alison watched him from the window. What an odd duck, she thought to herself. In all the time he'd come into the store, they'd never exchanged more than two words, if even that. Yet they'd known each other for years. She saw he was still driving that ancient Mercedes with the vanity plate, SETS4U.

~~~

The afternoon was turning out to be a telethon for Jack. He'd just finished talking with the Sheriffs when Brenda Carson rang. He still hoped to hear from Laura and the Jaguar guy in Ventura was also supposed to call.

"Hi, Brenda, what's up?"

"Sorry to bother you at home, Jack, but I'm trying to wrap up things at the office."

Jack imagined how difficult that must be for her.

"Anything I can do to help?" he asked.

"I've been in touch with Mike's attorney. He's the estate executor. Right now, I'm just paying outstanding bills and informing all of our past customers. I was wondering about the funeral. Do you know when they'll release Mike?"

Release Mike, Jack thought, as if he were locked up somewhere.

"You'll have to talk with the Sheriffs, Brenda. My guess is they'll let you have him when they've finished with the investigation. What about his relatives?"

"I got in touch with his son," she said, her voice breaking slightly. "Real piece of work there. Only interested in the will. The ex-wife is on a cruise some-where. Haven't been able to reach her."

"It's a shitty world. You need any help at the office? I can come over."

"I'm okay. It's sweet of you to ask."

The lawyer should be handling all that crap instead of leaving it to poor Brenda, he thought, hanging up.

His phone rang immediately.

"Is this Jack Hunter?" an unfamiliar voice asked.

"Yes, and may I ask who you are?" Jack asked tightly.

"I'm Moony Williams. Eric Nystrom said you have an

XKE you wanted me to look at. That right?"

Jack relaxed and smiled.

"Yes, sir, Mr. Williams. When could you do that?"

Jack figured Williams would want him to trailer the car to his shop. Although just starting the damn thing and driving it there himself was more appealing.

"I can be there in twenty minutes. Just about to leave my daughter's place in Santa Monica. Stop by on my way back. You're on Pacific Coast Highway in Malibu, right?"

Jack gave him the house number. He couldn't believe his good luck. He grabbed a beer from the refrigerator and took it out on the deck. He'd no sooner settled in the chair when, to his disbelief, the phone rang. This time he recognized the caller ID.

"Hi, Laura, tried to call you earlier."

"I know. Rivers told me. So what's up?"

Jack detected a tone in her voice that warned he might be wise to watch his step. The truth was, she'd been sorely stung by Bradshaw's comment on her failure to follow up with Hume's parole officer and was still smarting, not that she hadn't deserved it.

"You okay?" he asked, innocently blundering into the minefield. "Sound a little stressed."

That did it.

"Look, Jack," she snapped impatiently. "I'm pretty busy here. So what did you want to know?"

He quickly updated her on everything that had happened since they'd last spoken with each other. Including his conversation with Alison Gordon and his recognizing George Overton.

"Have you talked with the Sheriffs?" she asked in a slightly friendlier tone. "Mike Eaton's homicide is their case."

"They don't seem to be all that interested in what I have to say. I wonder if they'd listen to you? See, I believe there's a connection here somewhere."

Dalton considered the possibility. Jack didn't know about the latest findings at the Hodges estate and the autopsy results. There well could be a connection between the two homicides. They could be looking at parallel investigations.

"Okay, I will call the Sheriffs. And please do be careful."

"I always am."

"I mean it this time, Jack."

Dalton rang off and he'd just picked up his beer to take a sip when the doorbell chimed. He raced to the front door and opened it. A short, wiry man with a rodent-like face stood there. Parked behind him was a beautifully restored Jaguar 3.8 sedan.

"I'm Moony Williams," the man said. "Where's the car?"

Jack shook his hand and told him to wait there while he opened the garage. A minute later the door rolled up. Williams walked in and circled the XKE a couple of times.

"Does it run?" he asked.

"I haven't tried to start it," Jack told him. "I replaced the battery and put in some gas."

Williams frowned at that and crinkled his nose as if he'd stepped in something a dog might've done on the floor.

"What kind of battery?"

"Twelve volts. I bought it at the service station along with a couple gallons of gas."

Williams slipped in behind the wheel and turned on the ignition. The engine fired to life with only a touch of the starter button. He sat listening to the sound as it settled into a steady idle. He killed the engine.

"Well, it runs," he said getting out of the car. "What else do you want to know?"

"I was planning on having it restored," Jack said, a little bemused. "Eric Nystrom suggested you check it out first."

Williams circled the car once more. Scowling with each step.

"You planning to show it?" he asked.

"I hadn't thought about showing it. Mainly I was going to just drive it."

Williams bunched his lips and nodded.

"Then I wouldn't do a show-type restoration. But here's what needs to be done. Carburetors should be rebuilt. Same with the ignition. Put in the correct battery. Retard the timing so it can run on the piss poor gas they sell nowadays. Replace all the hoses and belts. Fluids. That sort of thing. You have a nice car, Mr. Hunter."

He smiled for the first time.

"Thank you," Jack said. "Did you restore your Jag out there?"

"Daughter did most of the work. I'm getting too old."

Jack laughed.

"Do you think she could work on mine?" he asked.

"We're not too busy right now. She could pick it up tomorrow morning. Her name's Heather. Be here around nine."

Jack promised that he'd be ready and Williams drove off in his Jag. As he stepped back inside he realized that he hadn't checked his new-fangled security system to see who'd been at the door before he'd opened it. Yeah, he was always careful.

CHAPTER 22

Gary Rivenson worked for the Los Angeles Central Parole Office. He'd been Alvis Hume's parole officer at the San Fernando Valley unit when Alvis skipped town. Ironically, now everyone seemed relieved that the truant parolee had been found.

"His loss but our win," Rivenson joked. "Clears the record."

"Suppose that's one way to look at it," Dalton agreed, thinking gallows humor wasn't exclusive with cops.

"Thanks for calling back. I've been out of the office on vacation. Took my wife over to Hawaii for a couple of weeks. You ever been there?"

"No, but I hear it's supposed to be great."

"Actually, I'm sorry this happened to Hume," Rivenson said. "I do remember him now. Always reported in on time. Had gotten a job. Seemed to be making it."

"And where was he working?" Dalton asked. "Maybe I can get some more information from his employer."

"Private residence on Mulholland. Guy named Hodges. Real prick, yeah. Called him to confirm Hume's employment. Don't know if he still lives there. I checked it out after Hume stopped showing up. You want the address?"

Dalton's brain had slammed on the brakes at Hodges.

"Martin Hodges died in an automobile accident a few months ago," she said retrospectively. "In fact, there was a shooting at his place we're investigating."

"Didn't know about that," Rivenson said. "Kind of out of the San Fernando Valley loop since moving to Central. Also, been traveling a lot. If there's anything more you need, detective, you know where to find me."

Indeed she did, but right now she needed to find out what Jason had learned. She thanked the parole office and hung up.

"You won't believe this," she said to Bradshaw at his desk. "Alvis Hume went to work for Martin Hodges after he got out of prison."

"For how long?" Bradshaw asked.

"I imagine until he stopped showing up at the parole office."

"Guess he'd found a home, huh?"

Dalton ignored the comment.

"What was that parole officer's name," Bradshaw asked.

"Gary Rivenson. Used to work San Fernando Valley unit. Now he's with Central."

"Yeah, think I've met him. He'd sit in sometime at this jazz joint over in Burbank. Believe he played bass."

"Jason should soon be back from Corcoran," Dalton volunteered.

~~~

George Overton was distracted. He'd been that way all afternoon. Delay followed delay. Unnecessary takes. He'd lost control. And now it was going to cost him. They were running out of light.

"How many more setups do we have?" he asked the AD, squinting through his director's lens.

"Two more after this," the assistant director told him. "Medium shot with the talent and then a close up for the product."

"Shit, I'm already wide open," he said, noting the aperture reading. "What time's sunset?"

"You've got about ten minutes."

"Better get some lights ready," George decided. "Ten K and a couple of fives ought to do."

The AD ran off to find the gaffer to rig the lighting.

Spotting Jack Hunter earlier that morning had rattled George. His immediate and real fear had been that Jack would've recognized him. When Jack had given no sign of doing so, paranoia had cast its net over George. Convinced that Hunter's showing up couldn't have been a coincidence, he'd begun to obsess. Why was Jack here? Who had sent him? What was going on? More to the point, what should he do about it?

The agency creatives had waylaid the AD and were arguing with him about the lighting. They all looked over at George. The assistant director threw up his hands and then began walking back to the camera.

"They don't want lights," he reported to George. "Say it won't match the other takes. So what do you want to do?"

George shook his head and picked up the bullhorn.

"It's a wrap everybody!"

The agency producer beelined it toward George.

"Why are you calling a wrap?" she demanded. "There are two more shots."

"Lost the light," George told her, getting up from the camera dolly.

"Well, who's fucking fault is that?" she yelled. "I want another shoot day and it's on you!"

"You'll have to speak with Brian," George said quietly. "That's his call, not mine."

Brian Gordon had just parked his red Porsche Carrera at the location and was walking up.

"How'd it go?" he said to the group.

"Ran out of light," George said. "Agency's unhappy."

"Did you get what you needed?" Brian asked.

"Missed one with the talent," George shrugged. "Better off without it anyway. Product shot I can do at the studio tomorrow."

Brian looked at the agency producer.

"You okay with that?"

"Whatever," she said dismissively, and turned to the others. "Might as well go to dinner."

"Hang on a second, George" Brian said after they'd gone.

The two men walked over to where the Porsche was parked.

"It's not like you to miss a shot, George. Maybe your AD dropped the ball. You should have someone on staff to work with you exclusively. Would you be okay with that?"

George didn't say one way or the other.

"In fact, I've got a guy in mind," Brian continued. "Used to be an agency producer so he knows that side of the fence. Could be a good assistant director. I asked him to drop by today and talk with you. Jack Hunter. Did he show up?"

George's face took on a hard expression. He didn't know what game was being played but now he knew the players.

~~~

A shallow marine layer had defused the sunset leaving the ocean bleak and uninviting. Jack felt a chill and abandoned the deck for the cozier living room. He flicked on the TV for some news. A car chase on the 405 Freeway. They caught the guy at Long Beach. He turned the set off.

He was in a down mood. He should be excited. The Jag would soon be up and running. But events of a much greater importance overshadowed that of a car tune-up. His friend been murdered. He now knew the name of the creep who'd barged into his house and suspected that he and his crazy girlfriend hadn't come there for a drink of water. Then there was Alison Gordon's warning and Dalton's concern. Yet here he was watching car chases.

He'd better start paying attention. That had always been the key to his survival. Pay attention. Know what the hell's going on and how it's going to affect you. Both now and in the future. Pay attention!

George Overton came into focus. He should have introduced himself today, as Brian Gordon had suggested. Would've been interesting to have seen his reaction. Until that moment, all he had thought about Overton was what Alison had told him. He was a bad guy. Stay away from him. But then to have recognized him as the person who'd come into his home, well, that was a whole other story.

He decided to call Brian Gordon and make an appointment to see him tomorrow. Ask if George could be there, too.

~~~

Detective Rivers was less than an hour from LA on his way back from the state prison at Corcoran. It's a male-only facility with individual cells, fenced perimeters and armed coverage. Classified as minimum-maximum security, it offers Level IV housing with more staff and armed guards both inside and outside the installation. And for those who require a little extra protection from the other prisoners, there is the Protective Housing Unit. It's usually a calm area because the inmates there don't want to be moved. One violent incident did occur in March 1999 when three prisoners smashed Charles Manson's guitar.

Alvis Hume had been in general population during his stint at Corcoran. He'd kept his nose clean during his incarceration according to the records. Worked in the prison library along with his cell neighbor, Larry Bolt, who was serving ten years for second-degree murder. He'd killed his girlfriend in a car accident while driving drunk. He'd had prior DUIs. Good behavior and prison overcrowding got him released after five years. Word was, he'd been a big-time music producer before being incarcerated. Gossip always ran freely in the cellblocks.

Rivers had passed through Bakersfield and had just joined the 5 going up the Grapevine when a semi coming down the interstate on the opposite side suddenly veered to the left and crashed into the center lane divider, jackknifed and turned over, spilling its cargo and flinging wreckage everywhere. One piece whipsawed through the air straight at Rivers. He ducked and jumped the bike to the right with opposite steering avoiding the debris but the motorcycle went down, sending him and it skidding across the highway and over the embankment.

Rivers was knocked unconscious. His bike was totaled.

~~~

Jack was delightfully in hot water. Alison Gordon had called to invite him over to her place. They were now sitting half-submerged and half-naked in the Jacuzzi by the pool.

Alison lived in a house hidden up a small canyon near Will Rogers State Beach. It was an exclusive and close-knit neighborhood where everyone minded his own business. The setting was straight out of a Hollywood movie.

"Was that a good idea?" Alison asked with concern, sipping from her glass of wine. "I mean, going to the location."

"I found out who it was that came to my place so to me it was a good idea."

"And what more do you expect to learn now by going to Titan?"

"Won't know that until I get there."

"Be careful of George Overton," she said.

Jack grunted and took in the surroundings.

"Nice home," he said.

"My dad left it to me. Same with the bookstore. Brian got the money."

"What business was your dad in?"

"He owned a recording studio."

"Must've been successful."

"Terribly so. A lot of drugs exchanged hands there."

Jack had confided to Alison the recent unsettling events in his life. He'd realized he could have been making a mistake but decided to take the chance. After all, she could be involved. That little red light of his seemed to be burning in overtime lately.

"David Hodges was a regular at the studio," Alison said. "Brought in the big names. Translate that into big bucks. After he died, Martin took over. I was away at school. Brian had finished at UCLA and was working at the studio. His interest had been in films but you take what you can get. He and Martin became friends."

"Mutual interests?" Jack said. "The cars, I mean."

"Yeah, the cars. Martin was basically a turd. Well, a flashy turd. He liked to show off. Porsches. Throw money around. Treated women like they were party favors. I think he was probably a sociopath."

"And your brother put up with all that?"

"He was fascinated by the lifestyle. And, of course, there were the cars."

Jack refilled both of their glasses.

"How did Brain come to own the production company?" he asked.

"Like I said, he'd majored in film. Martin put up some money. They formed Titan. Named it after what's supposed to be a bright spot on Saturn's moon."

They sat in silence for a minute.

"And you lived here?" he asked. "This was your house?"

"No. It was one of dad's investments, along with the bookstore. We lived in Sherman Oaks when Brian and I were born. Mom had an affair with her yoga teacher and got pregnant. Dad divorced her. And when her baby came, the guy split. Now we had a little half-sister, Joyce Stanley. Mom's maiden name was Stanley. It was confusing."

Jack could empathize. His childhood had also been

confusing.

"Dad took care of them. Got them an apartment in Hollywood. As kids we visited a lot. But he and mom never got back together."

"Where's Joyce today?"

"Could be anywhere. She works for an international security agency. Kind of a hush-hush outfit. Sounds exciting. She speaks eight languages."

"Do you ever hear from her?"

"Sometimes. I recently visited her in New York. She has places all over."

Alison looked over to Jack.

"Shall we get out?"

"Sure."

They both stepped from the Jacuzzi and Jack looked around for a towel to dry off. Alison ran her tongue over his nipple.

CHAPTER 23

H erb Thacker drove the Mercedes into the lot behind the photography studio. He noticed George Overton's truck and parked next to it. There were several items in the car trunk, one being the crow's cage, needed for the mass. He went inside to get some help.

Chris Parker was the inductee to the group and met Herb at the back door of the studio. Actually, to become a member of Satanism, you only needed to fill out a form and pay the annual fee up front. Herb had cut him some slack on the payment since Chris had volunteered his studio for the night's performance.

George and Cass were sitting on a sofa in the reception area and having a glass of wine. Cass looked to be orbiting the moon. Herb suspected several lines of coke had gotten her there. The high priest and beneficiary of the proceedings waited in the studio, dressed in a black robe.

"Thought there'd be others here," Herb said. "This it?"

"Have to do," George told him.

"Well, it's a small bird," Herb said. "Some stuff out in the car. You want to give me a hand?"

They brought in two cardboard boxes containing black candles, a chalice, a couple of boxes of different colored salt, Herb's black robe and a copy of the Satanic bible.

The bible illustrates rituals, rites, holy days and nine statements of the Devil. It's split into four different parts. Lucifer, designated by air. Satan, fire. Leviathan, water. And Belial, Earth. Each has its own environmental symbol.

Herb went back for the crow's cage.

Chris Parker was chatting up Cass when he returned. He left the cage with them in the reception area and went into the studio where he drew a pentagram on the floor with the salt. Candles were placed at each point. When he was finally satisfied with the diagram, he moved some studio light stands around. He decided that keying the scene from what would be camera left would give a dramatic effect. Of course, he'd have to clear that with George, who he had to admit was a little more expert about all things concerning lighting.

At present, however, George's concern was with what was going on with Cass. She and Chris had blown two more lines of cocaine and were now solidly standing on the moon's surface. Not only that but Chris had roving hands and had run them up Cass's shirt. George felt his own hand slip into his pocket where he kept his knife.

"Let's get dressed," Herb called, putting on his robe.

"C'mon, Cass, put your tits back inside," George said, glaring at Chris. "It's ShowTime."

Cass got to her feet, steadied herself, and walked into the studio.

"Stand over here," Herb told her, indicating the western point of the pentagram. "And George, you take the opposite side. Chris, you're down from Cass. I'll be across from you with our guest of honor at the top."

Thus, the five points of the pentagram were stationed. Five was an evil number.

They all got into position and Herb began reciting the passages from the Satanic Bible. When he'd finished, he went into the reception area to retrieve the birdcage.

The mass called for a black bird to be killed at this point in the ceremony and portions of its body distributed among the members.

"Cass, you remove the bird," Herb intoned, opening the cage door.

Cass giggled and stuck in her hand.

The crow crouched at the ready, its black eyes burning with furor. Cass fumbled trying to reach for it. With blinding speed and an angry *caw*, the crow drove its beak into the tender part between her fingers like a nine-penny nail struck with a two-pound hammer.

Cass screamed and jerked back her hand, taking the cage with her and sending it flying. The cage hit the floor, bowling over three candles before it stopped rolling with the door facing up. The bird was out in a flash.

"Goddammit!" George cursed, ducking the flapping wings and slipping down on the salt.

The high priest, wide-eyed and startled, stepped back into a light stand, knocking it to the floor where it landed with a popping crash as the bulb exploded scattering sparks every which way.

"Watch the light!" Chris yelled too late.

Cass sucked at her punctured finger and bounced on her feet while Herb shouted for a fire extinguisher. A paper backdrop had caught fire.

The crow had perched on another light stand. George swept at it with his knife. It fluttered vertically out of reach before spotting the open skylight.

Gone. A black bird into the black night.

~~~

Detective Jason Rivers had been airlifted to the UCLA hospital in Westwood. He was resting in ICU for observation. Dalton now stood in the emergency room talking with the ER doctor who'd initially treated him.

"The officer suffered a back injury that has led to some partial paralysis," he said. "The neurologist feels that it's only a temporary condition. No damage to the spinal cord."

"God," Dalton gasped, putting her hand to her mouth. "Will he be all right?"

"Could be that it's just sprained muscles. Although they're painful, these types of injuries usually heal themselves given time. Also, he has a mild concussion.

Lucky he was wearing a helmet. He'd regained consciousness before the paramedics arrived, which is a good sign. That's also how we knew to call you."

"How long will he have to stay here?" she asked.

"The next twenty-four hours will tell."

"Can I see him?"

"It would be better to let him rest for now. Tomorrow should be good."

Dalton felt devastated. This was all her fault. She'd suggested Rivers go up to Corcoran. Bradshaw was right, why the hell hadn't she just have him call instead of driving? How was she to have known he would ride the damn stupid motorcycle? Did he even own a car?

She walked to the lot and got in her Porsche. Well, at least Rivers was awake. That was one good thing, wasn't it?

Bradshaw had already left the station when the news had come in about the accident. His phone had gone to message. Now she'd give him another try. He answered on the first ring.

"What's up, Laura?"

"Didn't you get my message?"

"Just came through the door. Hadn't checked."

"Jason had an accident. He's at UCLA. It could be serious."

She then explained what had happened, the extent of his injuries and what the doctor had told her to expect.

"I don't know what to do, Tom," she said desperately. "I shouldn't have sent him."

"There's nothing for you to do, Laura. Stop blaming yourself. It was an accident. Where are you now?"

She told him that she was in her car at the lot.

"Are you okay to drive?"

"Of course I am," she said.

"Good. Go home. I'll see you in the morning."

Soon as they'd hung up, Bradshaw got on the horn with the hospital.

~~~

Traffic crawled over the Santa Monica Mountains to the Valley. Dalton got off the 405 at Ventura Boulevard. She was at a loose end. She ought to go home as Bradshaw had told her. But what then? Sit on her patio by herself with a glass of wine and stare into the darkness? Beat up on herself some more about Jason Rivers? Worry if the coyotes will get her cat? She headed for the station.

The detectives room was empty. She got herself a cup of coffee from the machine and settled at her desk. There was a message from Gary Rivenson. It wasn't all that late. Besides, he'd left his home number. She picked up her phone and dialed.

"Rivenson," a sleepy voice answered.

"Hi, this is Detective Dalton. You called. Hope I didn't wake you."

"Not at all," he yawned. "Actually, you did me a favor. I'd dropped off watching a reality show, Swamp Justice. Ever catch it?"

"Probably comes on after my bedtime. So what was it you wanted?"

"I remembered something about Alvis Hume. That job he had. Person that got it for him was another ex-con he'd met in Corcoran. Larry Bolt. Apparently, Bolt was in tight with the people who owned the estate."

Dalton took a breath. This could be huge.

"Do you have an current address on Larry Bolt?"

"Call Bill Tyson. He was Bolt's parole officer. Still works the Valley, if he hasn't retired."

"Thanks so much. Enjoy Swamp Justice."

She hung up and went to refresh her coffee. Three cups later she'd gathered quite a bit of information on Larry Bolt. Most of it was routine – occupation, arrest record, trial, sentence. Except for Hume's relationship with Bolt and his with the Hodges. She'd get on that in the morning with Tyson.

There was one small item of particular interest she'd discovered on Bolt's arrest sheet. He had once been brought in for animal cruelty. As far as she could tell, no charges had ever been filed or if so, were dropped. That set her off. She could never forgive anyone brutish enough to hurt a defenseless and trusting animal, no matter what their reason. People killing each other was one thing. At least that was explainable, so the psychiatrists say.

Then, naturally, another thought came to mind. The animal skeletons at the Hodges. Put together by an amateur, according to the medical examiner. Where had he gotten those animals? Had they been pets? Taken from a neighbor's backyard and put to death just to satisfy some twisted interest in anatomy? Was that what the animal cruelty charge had been about? As a possibility, it worked.

Moreover, the same person quite possibly had carved up Alvis Hume!

She went on the net and searched for anatomy. A ton of information on humans but nothing useful. She narrowed it down to animal anatomy. This looked more interesting. Still, nothing absolute. Okay. For the hell of it, she added *amateur* to the title. That opened another world. Clicking on a few sites, she came to a page for morbid anatomy which offered enough examples to turn your stomach. Stuffed squirrels, rats, snakes, articulated skeletons, skulls, pickled things in mason jars you'd never want to look twice at. But best of all, it listed a secret science club with a website address.

So much for secrecy. She went to the club's site, found a comment section and typed in a query. *Trying to locate Larry Bolt in Los Angeles. Have his dog skeleton. Need to return it.*

Five minutes later, a reply popped up – the address for the Hodges estate. It was time for her to call it a night.

CHAPTER 24

Jack had taken a dawn run along the beach. The tide was out and the sand packed hard enough to make for nice footing. From his house to Malibu Colony and back was a little over three miles which, at a quick pace, would really get your heart started. He cooled off the last hundred yards.

The shower beneath the deck had only a cold water line, not a place to linger. He grabbed a towel and dried, rubbing vigorously to peak the circulation. It felt good.

Alison Gordon was a puzzle. He had spent half the night and this morning trying to figure her out and was no closer to doing so than when he'd started. And when did this puzzle start? The first date, if you will. After the party at her brother's. That strange business at Dan Tana's. Then her abrupt kiss. And now last night she'd come on to him again only to immediately break it off. Was there a game being played here, and if so, what was it? She had invited him over. The hot tub had been her idea. All was well, up to a point.

In both incidents they'd been discussing her family. So what was going on there? Obviously, more than she was willing to tell. And apparently, disturbing.

Moony Williams's daughter should be coming soon for the Jaguar. He went inside to dress.

Thirty minutes later, the doorbell rang. This time Jack checked to see who was there before opening the door. A fair-haired woman with bright blue eyes who looked little like Moony Williams stood at the entrance.

"Hi, I'm Heather Williams," she greeted with a smile. "Are you Jack?"

"Yes, would you like to come in?"

"Thanks but if you'll just show us the car, we'll get it back to the shop."

She motioned toward a beautifully restored MGA, red with a tan leather interior. Its top was down and a man sat waiting in the driver's seat.

"You do the car?" Jack asked.

"Few years ago. It's the shop driver. That's Klaus. He's my body man."

Klaus gave a cool little wave. Jack returned it.

"I'll drive your Jag," Heather said.

Jack raised the garage door and the two of them went inside. Heather slowly walked around the car, stooping to look in the wheel wells.

"Nice," she said.

"How long do you think you'll need to keep it?" Jack asked.

"Unless we find something nasty, which I doubt, then maybe five days? I'd like to rebuild the carburetors and ignition, reset the timing and just go over all the mechanics. One other thing you might want to consider is having it really well-detailed. Paint, interior, the works. I've got a great guy. Not cheap but worth it."

"Let's do it," Jack said.

Heather backed the XKE out and onto the drive. Jack watched as she nosed up to PCH to wait for a break in the traffic, the little MGA trailing behind. It was a pretty sight.

~~~

Herb Thacker's houseguest had awakened with a ravishing appetite. He'd missed lunch the day before and there'd been no chance of catching dinner last night. Normally that wouldn't have been a problem. He hadn't eaten right for days. Chalked it up to whatever was ailing him. But this morning was different. And he welcomed the change.

Herb was still sound asleep in the other bedroom.

The guest got out of bed and tiptoed to the kitchen where he hoped to rustle up something, even a bowl of cereal would be nice. He wasn't much of a cook but if there were some eggs, he thought he could manage to scramble them. Nothing in the cupboard. The refrigerator was bereft of eggs. Something on a shelf wrapped in cellophane that'd grown a fuzzy mantle. Six-pack of beer. Half bottle of white wine. He looked in the freezer compartment. Only thing there was a frosty human finger.

~~~

Cass's eyelids were sealed shut. She scrunched them even tighter in hope of silencing the slamming trip-hammers in the back of her head. Her hand throbbed painfully.

"You gonna lay there all day?" a gruff voice asked from the distance.

She managed to pry open her eyes and saw George standing stark-naked at the foot of the bed. He'd just gotten out of the shower.

"Rise and shine, sweet cheeks," he said. "I have to leave for the studio in a minute."

She flopped over onto her tummy.

"How's your hand?" George asked.

"It hurts," Cass sobbed into the pillow.

"Get your lazy ass up and put something on your damn hand," George barked, "then get dressed. I want you to come with me this morning."

~~~

Dalton and Bradshaw had arrived almost together at the hospital, the head of Homicide just stepping out of his car when Dalton's Porsche swept into the lot. He waited for her to park and then the two of them went to the front desk, where they were given Detective Jason River's room number. Jason was sitting up in bed when they walked in.

"Lo, Lazarus lives," grinned Bradshaw.

"How are you, Jason," Dalton asked anxiously.

"Little achy. Tired. Otherwise, fine."

"The doctor was worried that you might've had a concussion," Dalton said.

"I think I was knocked out in the crash. I mean, I must've been because the last thing I remembered was the bike going down. Next thing I knew I was on the side of the road. They were being cautious about the concussion. Tests didn't show anything."

"What about the back?" Bradshaw asked.

"Nothing broken. They've given me some stuff for the pain."

"You're one lucky S.O.B., I hope you know that," Bradshaw told him. "Jesus Christ, riding a damn motorcycle halfway up the state?"

"It's a very efficient means of transportation, sir."

Bradshaw looked out the window and shook his head. Efficient means of transportation, his ass, he thought.

"What'd you learn up there?" he asked, turning back to Rivers.

"Much of it we could've found out from here, as you probably expected. But there were a few really interesting pieces of information."

"Go on," Bradshaw said.

"I didn't talk with the warden and the records department had nothing outstanding about Hume, meaning no infractions like fights or contraband dealing, so he made early parole. But one of the guards had an interesting take on how he could've been such a good boy. The other cons stayed clear of him. I asked why and he said they were afraid of the evil spirits."

Bradshaw laughed.

"You're kidding," he said. "Evil spirits?"

"Not kidding at all. I told him what had happened to Hume and also about the occult interest. He said that there were three of them practicing Satanism. They were within their rights on freedom-of-religion grounds. Word got around that they were devil worshipers. Could cast spells, that sort of thing. Turned out to be the best protection they could've had."

"That's amazing," Bradshaw marveled. "Did he say who the other two cons were?"

"Jules Wynn, he's still there doing twenty to life for strangling his business partner. The other one was kind of the ringleader, Larry Bolt. He'd been in for second-degree murder. He made parole right after Hume. But now get this. He was a boy wonder in the music industry. Don't know where he is now."

"I might be able to help on that," Dalton said.

She filled them both in on the lead she'd gotten from the parole officer last night.

"I'll give Bill Tyson a call as soon as we get back," she said to Bradshaw.

"Wasn't there a housekeeper at the Hodges place you were trying to locate?" he asked.

"Yeah, no luck so far," Dalton told him. "The lawyer who's handling the probate has been away. I'll call his office again. Also, this Tyson guy might know something."

"Doctor say when you're getting out, Jason?" Bradshaw asked.

"Probably this afternoon. They want to make sure about the concussion."

"Good. Stay home tomorrow and rest. Take it easy. And buy yourself a car before you come back to work. No more fucking two-wheel coffins."

~~~

Emilio Zaragoza got George Overton's voice mailbox. He didn't bother to leave a message. Instead, he called Brian Gordon at Titan Films.

"Well, George is on his way here, Sheriff," Brian said.

"Has a pickup shoot in our parking lot. Probably why his phone's off. He stays pretty focused when he's working."

"Okay," Zaragoza said. "No big deal. I'm following up on a question I'd asked earlier. Maybe I'll catch George later."

Zaragoza thanked him and said goodbye. He didn't bother asking Brian to tell George that he'd called. He would do that in person when they met. He had dressed in his uniform for the occasion. Something unnerving about a lawman's outfit to the bad guy.

On a good day, the drive from the Sheriffs office to the studio would take a little more than a half-hour. This morning, however, he'd need the other half, as well. But he had always found the freeway to be a good venue for thinking.

He was certain that Overton was involved with Mike Eaton's homicide. To what extent he couldn't say. He'd been at the scene. He had lied. He had the means, as much as anyone would've had them. But what was the motive? From the way Eaton had died, you could consider it to be a hate crime. Would his having been gay had anything to do with that? George Overton's comment at West Hollywood suggested that he might have a problem with gays. Still, why go to all the trouble of driving out in the desert and setting fire to the car, if you were homophobic? Pretty risky. The last place Eaton was said to have gone was to Topanga. Maybe someone saw him. Might be a smart idea to canvas the entire neighborhood with a picture of Eaton and the Honda. Good job for Deputy Brinkley.

All right, they'd split it up, he decided after feeling a tinge of guilt. He wouldn't mind dropping in on Alison Gordon anyway. Traffic halted at the junction of the 405 and the 101.

CHAPTER 25

"George is shooting out back," Brian Gordon told Jack. "Pick up he'd missed on location when the light dumped."

Jack had phoned Gordon earlier and had been delighted to learn that Overton would be at the studio. He'd asked him not to mention anything about his dropping by.

"Supposed to have been a quickie but as you can see," he continued, "the thing's grown into a major production. That's George for you."

Jack peeked through the glass window in the door to the parking lot. A couple of people milled around. Crewmembers. He saw the two women who'd been arguing at the location in Santa Monica. Overton sat on a dolly fidgeting with the camera. A huge piece of white seamless paper had been strung up on a couple of grip stands for a backdrop. An uncomfortable-looking man dressed in new jeans stood in front of it. Jack recognized him as the agency writer. And to his surprise, next to the writer was the feral-eyed woman who'd come into his house with George. She wore a bandage on her right hand.

"They're getting ready to film," Brian whispered. "We better wait here until the take is over."

Jack could hear what was being said outside on the set.

"The light's in my eyes," Cass complained. "I can't see."

George looked up from the camera eyepiece and motioned to the crewmember to adjust the reflector. The light reflection vanished from Cass's face.

"You don't have to see a damn thing, Cass, just feel

him, " he said. "And no quick moves. Real sexy-like. This is the money shot, remember. We're tight on his crotch. Cass, slowly run your hand down inside the front of the jeans when I say 'action'. And leave it there until I say you can remove it."

"It'd be better if I could use my other hand," Cass whined. "I'm right-handed, you know. I have to stand all funny to reach in with my left."

"Goddammit, then take off the bandage and use your right hand! Let's get this thing done!"

Cass carefully removed the gauze from her hand, her injury apparently well on the mend, and swapped sides with the writer.

"The light doesn't bother me from over here," she said cheerfully.

"Everybody ready?" George called. "Camera's rolling... speed ... and ... action!"

Cass slid her hand down into the jeans. The writer's eyes bulged momentarily.

"And ... cut! Beautiful! That's good, everybody. We can wrap now."

Jack and Brian opened the door and went outside.

"George," Brian called. "Got a minute? Want you to meet someone."

George turned to see Jack Hunter approaching with a goofy smile on his face.

~~~

Zaragoza had finally reached Venice Boulevard and to his joy, discovered the zoned parking space next to the building was empty. He stuck a sheriffs-official-business sign on the dashboard and went inside.

Sarah with the striking green eyes was seated at the reception desk.

"Sheriff Zaragoza," she smiled. "What brings you here?"

"Oh, just in the neighborhood," Zaragoza said, returning the smile. "Actually, I was hoping your director might be in. George Overton?"

"Aren't you the lucky one," she said. "You should buy a lottery ticket today. George is filming on our parking lot. You can go straight through if you want. George is a popular guy. Already another person here to see him. He's with Brian now."

Zaragoza thanked her and walked down the hall to the back.

~~~

George concentrated on a breathing technique he'd long ago learned to slow his heart rate. He had things pretty much in hand but Cass was verging on meltdown.

"This is the guy I mentioned," Brian beamed. "George, meet Jack Hunter. Jack used to be a producer at Gaysome Hough."

Jack stuck out his hand, the lopsided grin still on his face.

"Glad to meet you, George," he nodded. "You know, you look kind of familiar. Have we ever worked together?"

George remained silent.

"No, on second thought, I don't believe so," Jack continued. "Must've been somewhere else."

Cass was thunderstruck with fear. She suddenly gathered herself up and struck out for the building.

Emilio Zaragoza opened the back door just as she was about to reach for it.

"Why, Mrs. Overton," he said. "What a pleasure."

Cass gave a little whimper and pushed past.

"Have a nice day, ma'am," he called after her.

A calm came over George as the sheriff walked toward the group. He understood now what was going on. He'd been betrayed. And his Judas was standing at his side. How it had all come about he had no idea. The day Martin had introduced Brian Gordon to the others he'd known the punk was a loser. Would never be a real member. Didn't have it in him. He was just a faggot party boy looking for a thrill. Well, he'd gotten more than he'd bargained for. The problem was, he had seen a couple of things he shouldn't have. Stupid fucking thrill seeker! Maybe that was what this thing right now was all about. Turning the cops onto him for some past shit and then being there for the kill had to be one humungous thrill. Son of a bitch! He reached in his pocket for his knife.

He was good with a knife. First, he'd take out the sheriff. Quick thrust to the chest, spin him around and grab the gun out of his holster. Then shoot that meddlesome Jack Hunter. Brian would be the last. Blow his fucking head off. No time for niceties.

But the knife wasn't there!

He remembered. He'd removed it before the last take. Kept getting in his way whenever he squatted around the camera. He involuntarily glanced at the dolly. There it was on the seat.

Zaragoza caught the movement and looked over himself.

"How're you doing, George?" he said, placing a hand on Overton's shoulder. "Tried to call you earlier but couldn't get through. Brian said you were working so I thought I'd drop by."

"What can I do for you, Sheriff?" Overton asked tightly.

"Just had a tiny question about where you lived in Arizona," Zaragoza said. "No biggie. Tying up loose ends is all."

He walked over to dolly and, taking a handkerchief from his pocket, picked up the knife.

"Man, that's one nasty looking piece of business," he said. "Yours?"

"No, not mine," George lied. "Found it on the dolly this morning. Think it must belong to one of the crew from yesterday. Going to give it to Sarah. She can call around."

"Uh-huh," Zaragoza nodded, examining the knife. He flicked open the blade. "Doesn't seem to be very practical. More like a pig sticker."

"Wouldn't know," George said.

"If I'm not mistaken, this appears to be a blood stain around where the blade folds."

"Again, I wouldn't know."

"Tell you what, George, I'm going to hold onto this knife. Sarah can find its owner later."

He pulled a plastic evidence bag from his pocket and put the knife in it. George's mouth went dry.

"What was it you wanted to ask about Arizona?" he hemmed, then cleared his throat.

"Ah, it's not important," Zaragoza smiled. "Least not for now. I best be going. Got a busy day ahead."

"Hold up, Sheriff," Jack said. "I'll walk out with you."

When they'd gotten on the sidewalk, Jack stopped and turned to Zaragoza.

"What the hell's going on?" he demanded to know. "Those two are the same people who came into my house. I told you about them before and you just ignored me. Now here they are right in front of us. And another thing, I have some real suspicions about Overton having had something to do with Mike."

"So do I, Mr. Hunter, and I'd appreciate you leaving them to me. Have a good day."

~~~

Brian had gone inside the building with the agency people.

"We'll send everything to your editor," he told him. "I think that product shot today is great. Bet you win an award for the commercial."

"It was George's idea," the art director said.

"Well, that's George for you."

CHAPTER 26

Alison Gordon had opened the shop late that morning. Actually, she hadn't felt like coming in at all. It'd been like that lately. She didn't know what was wrong but of one thing she was certain. Whatever it was had started the day Jack Hunter had asked about Aleister Crowley. Time had jumped back and she was having a hell of a time catching up.

The night of that horrible party at Martin Hodges' now replayed itself at every unguarded moment. Revealing memories she'd thought forgotten. Why do people do this to themselves? This was supposed to have been tamped down for good by all those visits with her psychiatrist. Two sessions each week for over a year.

She stopped thinking about it and went next door to the coffee shop and brought back a large cup of Jamaica-Me-Crazy brewed from expensive Blue Mountain beans, a small luxury she allowed herself.

The memories were waiting when she returned.

~~~

She'd gone to the party on a lark. Her brother hadn't come out yet. He'd thought that having her on his arm, so to speak, would offer a little cover. The idea appealed and the fact that she was his sister kind of made it even more of a hoot.

Brian had worn a white dinner jacket and she'd picked out a revealing little thing from a Beverly Hills boutique. They looked hot.

Martin Hodges had met them at the door and immediately went out to inspect Brian's new car, a red Porsche 911 which her brother couldn't afford but had leased anyway. She'd left them to their fun and went inside. Most of the guests were already there.

A Hispanic woman had offered her a glass of champagne. Her name was Esther. She explained that she was the housekeeper and worked days but Martin had asked her to help for the evening. Esther had seemed upset. Perhaps it was because she'd had to stay late.

She'd wandered around. There were these awful animal skeletons in one room. She'd asked Esther about them. And learned that a friend of Martin's had made the dreadful things. In fact, he was at the party. Larry Bolt. More so, he'd worked for Martin's dad and had recently gotten out of prison.

Brian and Martin had finally joined the party.

She'd had a second glass of champagne and Martin had introduced her and Brian to the other guests. He didn't mention that they were brother and sister. A few of the men had paid her suggestive glances but one had seemed more interested in Brian. Herb Thacker, the little worm. Martin had put his arm around her waist.

Someone had produced a packet of cocaine. And then another. George Overton had arrived with a doe-eyed creature named Beth who'd given the impression that she'd rather be anywhere than there. She was beginning to empathize with Beth. She to went to look for Esther.

A man had relieved Ester and was now serving champagne. Alvis Hume. He was a shifty sort.

As night fell, the shadows had awakened with debauchery and the party had changed course. Raucous voices spewed and raunchy conversations sprang up. Groping. One couple even had had sex against the wall of an adjacent room. She'd looked around for Brian but couldn't find him.

Suddenly, George Overton had punched Alvis Hume in the face. Everyone laughed. He and Herb Thacker had led the poor man from the room. She could hear them shouting harshly at him. And then a scream.

She'd run from the house to the courtyard and discovered Beth there and in tears. The woman had been inconsolable. Unable to help and not knowing what else to do, she'd called for a taxi to take her home.

The next day she'd confronted her brother. He'd seemed nonplused. When she'd asked about the scream, he'd said it was just a party.

~~~

She had to pull herself together and stop bringing up the past. There was nothing she could do to change it. How many times had the psychiatrist said those same words? At $200 a session. She lit a cigarette and began to rearrange some of the bookshelves.

Still, she couldn't understand why she had behaved the way she had with Jack Hunter. Here was a guy she could make a go with. Now he probably thought she was just another nutcase like half the women in town. Maybe she ought to call her doctor for an appointment.

But she wasn't crazy. A bad thing *had* happened that night. And Brian had known. She'd never suspected that he'd been involved in the actual act but he'd been there. Of course, he'd denied it. She'd always been able to tell when he was holding back. Did his denial even matter in the end?

She finished straightening the books and happened to look out the window as Herb Thacker's old Mercedes passed by.

~~~

Bill Tyson had just pulled a couple of Florida vacation brochures from his desk when the phone rang.

"Tyson," he answered, shuffling through the folders with one hand.

"Mr. Tyson, this Detective Laura Dalton at Van Nuys Division. I need your help with one of your graduates.

Larry Bolt. Paroled in 2008 from Corcoran."

Tyson chuckled at the term 'graduate'.

"Give me a moment, detective," he said, putting the folders aside and making a few keystrokes on his computer.

"Serving ten years for second degree murder," Dalton added helpfully. "Got an early release after five."

"Yeah, here he is. What'd you want to know?"

"Anything you can tell me about him that's not written in his file. How did he strike you? Ever mention friends. That sort of thing."

Tyson was silent for a moment.

"Oh, yeah, now I remember him. He wasn't a likable bastard. Don't think he was one bit sorry about what he did. Pissed off that he went to jail, that's all. A lot of them are like that, though. Everything was all about him. Used to be a music producer. Liked to remind you of that."

This wasn't turning out to be as useful as Dalton had hoped.

"What about any friends?" she asked. "His job? Where did he stay?"

"Went back to his old job in the song business but apparently it wasn't the same. Had this pal who owned a big estate on Mulholland. He lived with him for a while. Moved to Topanga. Last place was in Marina del Rey. Finished with his parole there. Haven't heard from him since."

Dalton was disappointed in the last part. But now she knew that Larry Bolt and Alvis Hume had been on the estate during the same time.

"Oh, one more thing," Tyson added. "Don't know if it's any help. Larry was an amateur taxidermist. Always thought that was an unusual hobby. Stuffing things."

Dalton felt her pulse quicken.

"What kind of things?" she asked.

"Animals, I guess. Don't know if he got paid for it. You know, mount a deer's head somebody shot."

"So you never saw any of these ... uh, stuffed animals?"

"No, only one time he did bring in a snake skeleton. Rat snake, I believe it was. Whole snake, too. Not just part of it. Said he got all the flesh off with a chemical. Soaked it for a couple of days. Left the bones just like they'd come. All tidy and clean. And the kicker was, he knew the names of each and every one of those bones from head to tail."

This was good, Dalton thought. She had one more question.

"Did Larry Bolt ever talk about religion? I mean, his particular beliefs?"

"I'm not sure he believed in much of anything other than himself."

"Thank you very much, Mr. Tyson. This has been a big help."

"You're very welcome, detective. Good thing you caught me today. I'm leaving for Florida tomorrow. Taking my grandkids to Disney World. You ever been there?"

"I was in Florida once," she said, involuntarily touching the conch shell tattoo on her breast.

She next phoned Jason Rivers only to get his voice mail. This puzzled her because Rivers was supposed to have been released from the hospital yesterday afternoon. He should be home. In fact, she'd expected he would've called in himself by now. Maybe he was still asleep.

Tom Bradshaw sat down at his desk.

"Traffic was a bitch," he commented. "Hear anything from Rivers?"

"I just tried to get him but he's not answering his phone."

"Probably sleeping in," Bradshaw yawned. "Kind of tired myself. Late night."

"Don't tell me you were up watching Swamp Justice."

"What?"

"Just a joke. Look, Tom, I'm worried about Jason. If he got out yesterday like he said, then why hasn't he at least called to let us know?"

"Christ, he was wearing a helmet," Bradshaw said. "You don't suppose he had some sort of relapse, do you?"

He picked up the phone and dialed the hospital. Five minutes later and after being shuttled back and forth between departments, he was transferred to the nurses station at the Intensive Care Unit. Detective Rivers had been admitted late yesterday.

CHAPTER 27

H erb Thacker had put his cellphone on speaker. The volume wasn't nearly loud enough and the sound was always distorted. It was a cheap brand, after all. He should bite the bullet and buy a new iPhone but then Herb was a little on the cheap side himself. He strained to hear from where it lay on the passenger seat across from him. Still, having the phone on the lousy speaker was better than risking a ticket. The cops had cracked down lately on talking while driving.

"I'm due at the stage right now, George," he yelled. "We're just starting building the set and the goddamn filming begins tomorrow! Jesus Christ, these fucking people must be sleeping in their cars!"

Traffic was at a standstill on the 101.

"All I'm asking is this, Herb," George Overton's tinny voice crackled. "Are you with me or not?"

"Do what the fuck you want! You're going to anyway. Yeah, yeah, I'm with you."

"Good. That's what I wanted to hear. How's our priest this morning?"

"I think he should see a doctor."

"He was always a pussy."

~~~

"Mr. Rivers heart suffered a mitral valve prolapse," Dr. Donna Stabile explained. "That's when blood is forced back through the valve. Think of it as a leaky faucet."

Stabile was a resident cardiologist at UCLA. She'd returned Bradshaw's phone call.

"He'd temporarily lost consciousness yesterday and was taken to ICU," she continued. "I suspect the mitral valve deficiency was due to a congenital abnormality. Has he ever mentioned having heart murmurs?"

"Not to me, Doctor Stabile. Maybe it's on his medical records. You can check with the department."

"Thank you, we'll do that. Many people have murmurs. Often they simply clear up."

"What about Detective Rivers?" Bradshaw asked. "Is *his* going to clear up?"

"In his case, the mitral regurgitation was likely to have been prompted by the accident. Right now, we're taking temporary measures until we can determine if valve replacement surgery is necessary. My hope is for surgical repair rather than replacement, which is riskier. Another option is trans-catheter repair. It's a less intrusive procedure. It can reduce the severity of the damage and possibly lead to the valve remodeling itself. Mr. Rivers is a young man. He should be all right."

"When will you know for sure?" Bradshaw asked.

"That's all I can tell you for now."

Bradshaw hung up and looked at Dalton.

"I hope the fuck they know what they're doing," he said angrily. "This wait-and-see bullshit doesn't cut it."

"I'm so sorry, Tom," Dalton said sadly. "This should never have happened."

"Not your fault, Laura. I've already told you. Now, let's get to work. How do we find Larry Bolt?"

Dalton heaved a breath.

"I know," she said. "But I can't help it. I was the one who sent him up there."

"Larry Bolt?" Bradshaw prompted.

"Okay. His last known address was in the Marina," Dalton sighed. "Had a small apartment there. Got evicted."

"That's not much to go on. Any idea about where he might've moved?"

"Well, here's a dumb idea. He could have been living on the Hodges estate until Martin got himself killed and the place went on the market."

"Not so dumb, Laura. I doubt if there'd have been a lease involved so it would be a civil matter. Lawyer for the estate wouldn't have had any problem kicking his butt out. Maybe Ed Stone was back in town. Give him a call. Also, run down that apartment in Marina. If he was evicted, there has to be a record. Maybe the manager knows something about Larry Bolt that'd be useful."

~~~

Jack had driven into Beverly Hills for breakfast at The Pink Palace, aka, The Beverly Hills Hotel. He'd gone to the Fountain Coffee Shop and sat at the counter. Dress code was easier here. No jacket required. Just be sure your sweater was 100% pure cashmere.

The peach and green painted hotel had fallen out of popularity with celebrities during the brouhaha over the Sultan of Brunei's ownership but now things were once again running smoothly. And the soda fountain had never ceased to be a fun place to meet and eat. You'd arrived when the waitress knew what flavor of yogurt you liked and the chef gave you a wink.

He'd finished eating his perfectly scrambled eggs and reading the *LA Times,* which had an interesting story about the assassination of a government bigwig in Mexico City. He was now walking on a path through the tropically-planted rear area of the hotel where the bungalows stood, some renting for up to fifteen grand a night, when his phone rang.

"Jack, it's me," Dalton said. "Hope I'm not interrupting."

"Not at all. Just taking a stroll among the money trees."

"What?"

"I'm at the Beverly Hills Hotel," he laughed. "Decided to have breakfast here. Want to come over?"

"I have a question," Dalton said seriously. "I'm trying to get in touch with Ed Stone. He's apparently still away. Would you have any idea of where he might be?"

"Mike said he had a place up in Tahoe. Could be there. His office should have a number where he can be reached."

"You'd think so," Dalton said. "It seems he works out of his home and his calls go to voice mail. I left him a message but I'd like to get to him sooner."

"Brenda might have his number. What's up?"

"Just need to talk with him," Dalton told him, regretting that she hadn't thought of called Mike Eaton's office herself instead of involving Jack.

"Say, I want to run this past you," Jack said, himself now serious. "I saw the two people who came to my house again. George Overton. Remember I told you about him? It was at Titan Films. And his girlfriend was there, too. But here's what's bugging me. That county Mountie sheriff was there as well. But he doesn't seem to be all that interested. So what do you think?"

"I think he's probably doing his job, Jack. And you should stay out of it unless he asks for something. I mean it. We've been through this before so I know how you are."

Well, he *had* almost gotten the two of them killed awhile back in Key West.

"Funny about me staying out of it," Jack said. "Sheriff told me the same thing."

Dalton thanked him and hung up. He walked on past the bungalows facing Crescent Drive where he'd parked the Jeep. That was the cool place to park when you were just ducking into the hotel. He decided he'd drive over to Century City.

~~~

Brenda Carson had just finished speaking with Dalton when Jack knocked on the office door and came in.

"Hi, I was nearby and thought I'd see how you're

doing," he said.

"Your detective friend called me a few minutes ago. Wanted to know if I had Ed Stone's phone number in Tahoe. Now why would I have that?"

Guess she'll have to wait for him to call back, Jack thought to himself.

"Looks like you've got everything in hand," he said, taking note of all the boxes on the floor. "Kind of strange."

"Packed up and ready to leave," she replied. "Yeah, it is strange. Haven't found a new job but something will come along. Got to pay for the groceries, you know."

Jack smiled. He wondered if his real estate management office needed any help? Not really. He'd check anyway.

"There is this one thing," Brenda said. "A little scrap of paper stuck in Mike's blotter on his desk. Looks like it might be part of an address. I don't know if it means anything or not. Could've been there forever."

"You have it?"

"Here somewhere," she muttered, rummaging around in her purse. "I was about to toss out the blotter when I discovered it. Ah, here we go."

She removed a torn half of an envelope with something scrawled on the back and handed it to him.

Jack examined the scrap. The writing ran off the edge, as if it had been hastily scribbled down. The numbers were clear but the name was nearly illegible. Several syllables could be made out, though.

"Mike probably had to copy it over," she laughed. "He always wrote things down in a hurry and then couldn't make heads or tails of them. Poor Mike."

"You're right, it could be an address," Jack said. "Or maybe something else. Shipping number or vehicle registration. You say you don't know how long it's been there?"

"Could've been written the last day he was in the office or last Christmas. But I was thinking about the Topanga address. Remember? I wasn't sure at the time but maybe this has something to do with it. No way of telling. If it was an address, he probably put it in his phone anyway. Should I just toss it out, then?"

"You should give it to the sheriff," he said. "Let him decide. It might be important."

He gave her back the envelope, having memorized the name and number.

CHAPTER 28

D alton's phone chirped and she quickly picked it up, hoping it might be Ed Stone returning her call.

"Detective Dalton, this Emilio Zaragoza. I've been thinking about you."

"Isn't that a coincidence," she said. "I've been thinking of you."

"Well, I'm flattered."

Dalton laughed.

"I'm afraid it has only to do with business," she said. "I wonder if we might need to compare notes on a couple of homicides. We might be running parallel investigations."

"You must be a mind reader," Zaragoza said. "Lately, I've been wondering the very same thing. What do you have?"

She began with the shooting death of James Stirling, next went through the murder book on Alvis Hume, and finally brought him up to date on where they now stood.

"You believe this Larry Bolt is involved in Hume's homicide?" Zaragoza asked. "And with Eaton, as well?"

"I don't know about Mike Eaton but I do think his involvement with Hume has a bearing on what happened to your victim."

"Thing is, sounds like Alvis Hume was butchered," Zaragoza said. "Fatally stabbed and dismembered. My guy was burned. Different MO."

"That's true," Dalton agreed. "But there's this occult business to consider. My partner believes it's behind the killing of Hume. From what I've gathered about Mike Eaton's death, there was evidence found at the scene to support his suspicions. That true?"

"I gather you're talking about the salt. Actually, I

thought that was interesting, myself. I've done a little research on the occult. Believe me, tying that to a motive is one hell of a reach. Sure, death by fire. Ceremonial salt spread around. Victim tortured first. More like a bad movie script, I'd say."

"I agree it's a reach," Dalton said. "I'm trying to get in touch with the estate executor and find out if he has any information on Bolt. Thought it might be him on the phone when you called. There's one other thing about this case that disturbs me. You're acquainted with Jack Hunter, I understand."

~~~

This was turning out to be Brenda Carson's lucky day. Jack had swung by his Beverly Hills office to check on the potential address she'd given him. He'd have someone call the county records and find out who owned the residence. It was public knowledge so there wouldn't be any problem getting the information, just the hassle of dealing with officialdom.

However, the person who would've done that for him had just started her maternity leave this morning and would be gone for a generous three months. His manager had already set up some interviews with a temp agency. Jack recommended Brenda for the job. The manager figured she would probably want something permanent but gave her a call. She snapped it up.

"I don't know how to thank you, Jack."

She'd phoned Jack.

"Well, it's only temporary but it'll pay for the groceries."

"You can say that again," she giggled with relief. "Oh, I called the sheriff about that address thing."

"Zaragoza?"

"He was out so I left a message."

"I'm sure he'll get back to you."

She thanked him again and said goodbye. Jack returned his attention to the address.

"Who do we usually work with at records?" he asked. "I need to put a name on this house. Might be in Topanga."

"Give it to me," his manager said.

To his amazement of how easily someone who knew what he was doing could cut through bureaucratic red tape, Jack had gotten the owner's name of the house near Topanga State Park.

~~~

Alison Gordon had spent a good half-hour on the phone with her brother. Their conversation hadn't gone well and had ended with her hanging up on him. She felt badly that she'd behaved so immaturely and was about to call him back to apologize when Jack walked in.

"Good afternoon," he greeted, handing her a small potted plant. "It likes indirect light and not too much water."

"Why, it's a little orchid," Alison said with a surprised delight. "And what a lovely color!"

"Yeah, I saw it at a flower stand near my office. Thought you might like to have it."

She kissed him on the cheek.

"Everything all right?" Jack asked, noticing that her eyes were red.

Alison blinked back a tear before answering.

"It's my stupid brother," she said. "We just had a terrible argument on the phone."

"Want to go somewhere and have a cup of coffee? You can tell me about it."

"No, I'm okay here.'

She sat down in a chair near the door. Jack took a seat on the floor next to her.

"In case you haven't noticed," she said, "I think I'm losing my mind."

"For any particular reason?"

"Mainly, I'm worried sick about Brian."

Jack looked at her curiously.

"Are he and Dag having problems?"

Alison closed her eyes and shook her head.

"No, that'd be easy. This goes back a long way. But it's something I can't tell anyone about, so please don't ask."

Jack nodded.

"You and that sheriff were at Titan," she said suddenly.

"That's right. Brian wanted me to drop by. I didn't know the sheriff was going to be there, too."

He didn't say that he had more or less invited himself to visit.

"Turned out to be a surprise for everyone. Especially George."

"What are you trying to do, Jack?" she asked angrily. "George Overton is not a nice person, believe me. Definitely not someone you want to mess with. I've told you over and over."

"They're the ones who came into my house," Jack said. "Overton and that woman who was with him. And they both know that I know. The sheriff knows, too, but he's not talking."

"Is that all? Just that they came into your house? That's not exactly the crime of the century."

Jack paused a moment. He wondered whose side Alison was really on.

"I believe there's more to it," he said quietly.

They both sat without speaking. Finally, Alison turned to him.

"George had a big fight with Brian after you'd left," she said. "Told him he was through with Titan and to find himself another cameraman."

"That's interesting and I'm sorry. But there are a lot of

cameramen and directors in town. He shouldn't have any trouble filling Overton's position."

"That's not the point. George has never liked Brian."

She began to cry again. After she'd collected herself, she told him about the party.

"I didn't actually see what happened with that man, but I believe Brian did," she said when she had finished. "He's never come right out and said he was there at the time but certain things make me believe that he was."

"If what you've told me is true, he's in danger. Maybe you are, too. I think you should go to the police."

"There's no evidence."

"What if you called anonymously?" Jack suggested. "Cops are always getting tips. Might make them look harder at Overton."

"It was ages ago, Jack."

"Well, maybe I can dig up something."

"Jack, don't be foolish," she laughed harshly. "You'd be wasting your time." Alison stared blankly ahead.

"Jack, I'm tired. Think I'll close the shop and go home."

She got up from the chair and Jack pulled himself off the floor. She turned to him, taking his hands in hers.

"Want to come with me?" she said.

Jack hesitated.

"I don't blame you for not wanting to," she sighed. "Last time was kind of a bust."

"It's not that, Alison. I think I've found Aleister Crowley. I'm going to pay him a visit."

~~~

La Mer Arms in Marina del Rey was on a lot off Culver Boulevard the other side of US1. Put up in the seventies with the idea of cashing in on short-term tenancy from LAX and offering only basic amenities. Today, it verged on being a dump and amenities offered now were few if any.

Dalton had driven there after getting the address from Bill Tyson.

"I remember Larry Bolt," Max Cogan said. "Though he wasn't here very long."

Cogan was the manager of the housing complex. He was a stout man, solidly built and of East European ancestry. He wore black chino trousers and a white dress shirt. The top button was missing.

"He'd been in prison. Parole office sends ex-cons here sometime. All right with me as long as they don't cause trouble," Cogan continued.

"Did Larry Bolt?" Dalton asked. "Cause trouble?"

"No problems in that department."

"Then why was he evicted?"

"He stank up the place. I'd describe the odor but you being a lady, let's just say it was god-awful."

"You'll have to explain that to me," Dalton said.

"Larry played around with taxidermy," Cogan said. "Stuffed cats, dogs. Birds, if you can believe that. Nobody wanted the damn things. His apartment smelled like a zoo. Neighbors complained every day. One even moved out. I talked to him about it more than once. Finally, I told him either nix it with the stuffing or I was going to have him evicted. He just laughed. Told me where I could go. He'd finished his parole so I guess it didn't matter to him."

"Did he have any friends or anyone that came to see him while he lived here?"

"Yeah, there was one guy. Come by to pick him up. Larry didn't drive. They belonged to some club. What the hell was it? The Mendes Society, I believe. Maybe they were all taxidermists. James Sterling. That's who he was. I never forget a name."

~~~

Jack found the address about halfway up the road leading into the state park. He decided to leave the Jeep on the road shoulder rather than go down the drive. The house was a nondescript box, probably built in the late fifties, but it had a huge deck on the back with a to-die-for view. It'd be a teardown in a minute.

There didn't look to be anyone at home. He knocked on the door. Then knocked again, harder.

"Hello," he called out.

He finally heard footsteps approach from inside, the door latch rattled open, and an ashen-faced wrinkled man stood before him.

"What do you want?" the man demanded.

"Sorry to disturb you," Jack said. "Are you Mr. Thacker?"

"He's not here."

"Oh, then you must be Aleister Crowley."

The man stared at him.

"I'm Jack Hunter. I understand you were interested in buying my car. May I come in?"

The man stood silently for a moment, then turned away. Jack followed him inside. An odor of death met him as soon as he stepped through the door. He'd smelled it before.

The ancient memory rushed to the forefront ... his army patrol unit approached the darkened pockmarked house cautiously. He signaled with his hand for two men to cover each side of the doorway. He would be first to enter. The silence was complete. His senses placed on high alert. He pushed against the door gently with his gun barrel. Was the door booby-trapped? It swung open easily on its hinges and fanned out an unmistakable stench from the room. Eight bodies sprawled in various positions on the floor. Each had been shot in the head. An execution. Three were children. He backed out of the doorway. He snapped to the present. The horrific scene returned to that place in the mind where such things sleep until next awakened.

"You'd spoken with Mike Eaton on the phone about the Jaguar," Jack said. "He was going to show you some cars."

"You need to come back later," the man wheezed.

Jack noticed a mobile hanging from the ceiling in front of a rear window. He walked over to it for a better look. Bat skeletons, delicate and fragile, carefully attached to one another, wingtip to bony wingtip. Sensitive to the slightest disturbance, they circled in an airy ballet. He thought it was something out of hell.

"Hard to get the bones without breaking them. Bats have small teeth."

"Are you okay?" Jack asked the man, who had steadied himself against a chair.

Obviously he was anything but okay. His left arm hung uselessly at his side and a streak of drool ran down his cheek. He seemed frightened. Confused.

"I told them the bird was no good," the man said agitatedly. "Should've listen to me!"

"Would you like for me to call someone?" Jack asked, now concerned. "Do you need a doctor?"

"You know Mike Eaton, huh?" the old man laughed. "You better come back later."

Another strip of drool.

"I rave and I rape," he croaked. "I rip and I rend. Know who said that?"

Jack decided to get out of there. He started for the door.

"Know who said that?" the old man yelled after him hoarsely, his eyes red with rage. "Tell me who said that, motherfucker!"

Jack was now on the porch.

"Aleister Crowley said it, you poor excuse for a shit," the old man growled from the doorway. "Get the hell out of here!"

CHAPTER 29

"Esther Fellipe is who you want to talk with," Ed Stone said.

The lawyer had finally returned Dalton's phone call. She was at her desk in Van Nuys.

"Think she lives on Roscoe near Van Nuys airport. Her husband has a plumbing business. Probably under his name. I don't have anything with me. I'm still at the cabin."

Dalton jotted this down.

"Thanks, Mr. Stone," she said. "This is a big help. Sorry to have disturbed you."

"That's all right, detective. Good luck."

She'd need all the luck she could get she thought, hanging up. But who knows? This could be the lucky break in both cases.

"Any further word on Rivers?" Bradshaw asked, settling himself at the homicide table. He'd just come into the room.

"He's out of surgery and resting," Dalton told him. "According to the doctor, all is well. But it will take a few weeks before he's fully recovered."

"That's a relief," Bradshaw nodded. "What's up?"

"Just got off the phone with Ed Stone. He's the executor of the Hodges place I've been trying to reach."

"Yeah, yeah, I know who he is. What'd he say?"

Dalton took a moment to collect herself before answering. There'd been a tension building between the two of them ever since Rivers' accident. Neither one would admit to its existence but that didn't change the fact. Impatience on his part. A little cattiness on hers. It had to stop.

"Mr. Stone said that the housekeeper's name is Esther Fellipe," she said in a monotone. "She lives on Roscoe near Van Nuys airport. Her husband has his own plumbing business under his name."

She smiled.

Bradshaw returned it.

"Benny Fellipe," he said. "Good plumber. I've used him. Got his number here in my phone. Now, about you."

Dalton blushed. What the hell, she thought.

"I know you blame yourself for what happened to Rivers. My telling you that it wasn't your fault doesn't change anything. You've got to decide that for yourself but either way, live with it because your work's being affected, Laura. You're forgetting things you never would have before. For my money, you're the best detective in the whole department. Rivers is going to be fine. The doc said so. Okay? Let's focus on getting this damn thing solved."

He stuck out his hand and she took it.

"I'll call the Fellipe woman," she said. She knew her boss was right, although she felt like crying just the same. Or giving him a sock in the jaw.

~~~

Jack sat in the Jeep considering his next move. This one had been a total bust. In his defense, he hadn't had a plan when he'd walked into the house. He'd expected to find Herb Thacker living there, not a borderline pyscho. The Aleister Crowley ploy had backfired. Or maybe not. The problem was he didn't really know, did he?

But then who was the creepy geezer if he wasn't Herb Thacker? Oddly, the man didn't seem to be that old chronologically, if that made any kind of sense. His appearance was more that of a person ravaged by some horrible disease. He was definitely sick. And that stomach-turning smell that permeated everything!

He started the engine and began drifting down to

Topanga Canyon road. Passing the bookstore, he slowed enough to read the closed sign in the window. Alison had gone home. He should've taken her up on the offer.

~~~

George Overton walked with purpose along Sunset Boulevard in Hollywood. In his pocket was a new spear-point automatic knife with a four-inch blade he'd just bought at the store on Highland Avenue. He liked the way it felt against his thigh. How it moved with his muscles. A comforting presence ever at the ready. His next stop was a costume shop two blocks away.

~~~

The Fellipes lived in a neat bungalow set in one of the little pocket neighborhoods scattered across the San Fernando Valley. Upkept houses, tended lawns. Dalton had parked her Porsche on the street. Still she worried if it would be safe.

"I worked there until Martin had the accident," Esther Fellipe said, sipping from her coffee cup. "I would've quit sooner but Benny's business was slow and we needed the money. Things are a little better now but he has to be out so much. Guess that's the way it is these days if you're going to make ends meet."

She and Dalton were seated in the living room. When Dalton had earlier phoned, Esther invited her to come right then. Her husband was on a job and she wasn't busy. She gave the impression that she would enjoy some company,.

"When I read in the paper about the man who'd been shot, I didn't know if I should call the police. They said he was a burglar but he used to come there all the time. He was one of Martin's friends."

Dalton leaned back in her chair.

"You mean James Sterling," she said. "Do you remember seeing him at the house?"

"He was part of a group who would meet some nights during the month. He wasn't one of Martin's regular friends."

"What do you mean by *regular* friends?"

Esther blushed.

"He just came for the meetings. He was never at any parties."

"So you're saying James wasn't a close friend. What about those groups?"

"They weren't very nice people. I was afraid of them."

This was interesting, Dalton thought.

"Why were you afraid?"

"They were evil. They worshiped the Devil."

"Wait a minute," Dalton said. "You mentioned meetings just now. Is that what these things were?"

"Yes, they'd dress in black robes. It was scary."

"Were you afraid you might be harmed?"

"Sometimes people screamed. They hurt animals."

Dalton was starting to feel uneasy. And angry.

"The animals were sacrifices," Esther continued. "Usually a dog or cat. Once they killed a goat. They did it in the room above the garage."

"Did you actually see them kill the animals?" Dalton asked.

"I could hear what they were doing. They weren't quiet."

"What happened to the animal after it was ... sacrificed? Did they just toss it somewhere?"

"Larry made some of them into skeletons. He liked doing that."

Dalton sat quiet for a moment to take it all in. Answers to questions she'd earlier arrived at were starting to be confirmed.

"That would have been Larry Bolt who made the skeletons, right?" she said.

"Oh, how do you know Larry?" Esther asked in surprise.

"His name has come up once or twice in our investigation," Dalton said, "but anything you could tell me about him would be helpful."

"Well, Larry worked with Mr. David Hodges in his music business. He would come to the house sometimes. It was fun then. Larry played a guitar. I used to tease him. See, he was left-handed so everything was backwards for him. I told him it was like looking in a mirror. He and Martin became friends, although Larry was older. Would you like some more coffee? Also, I have some cinnamon rolls. Fresh from the store this morning."

"Thank you, Esther, but I'm fine," Dalton declined. She wondered if the poor lonely woman ever had company over.

"'Are you sure?" Esther smiled, getting up. "It's no bother."

"Well, some more coffee would be good," Dalton relented.

Esther beamed and went to the kitchen. She returned with a coffeepot as well as platter full of cinnamon rolls.

"Did you know that Larry had been in prison?" Dalton asked after Esther had settled.

"Yes, he got into trouble with the police over some girl. I never asked about what'd happened. David died while Larry was away. When he came back, he lived in the house for a while. Then Martin had the accident."

"I see, let's go back to some of the others who came around the house. Martin's friends. Do you remember them?"

Esther put her hand to her brow.

"Oh, my, there were so many when they had a party."

"Just the ones you know," Dalton smiled.

"Well, there was Brian. He and Martin were crazy

about cars. I liked him. He wasn't bad like the others. And George and Herb. George used to talk about Brian. Made fun of him. But mostly he picked on Larry's friend. Both of them did, George and Herb, they were always mean to him. I worried they might hurt him."

Dalton's felt her hair move on the back of her neck.

"Which friend was that, Esther?"

"Alvis Hume. He helped me take care of the house. Poor boy didn't know how to do much. He didn't stay long. I don't know where he went. One day he was here and the next gone. I think he just got tired of being picked on."

"He never said anything to you about George and Herb?" Dalton asked.

"Oh, no, he'd never talk to me. He was one of them. You know, devil worshiper."

Of course, Dalton thought to herself. Rivers had learned of the Satanist group Larry Bolt had formed with Hume at Corcoran. Bolt had brought him into this one. But why then had he been murdered? Was that the plan all along? A human sacrifice?

"Esther, did you ever go inside the room above the garage?" she asked. "You said that you heard what they did in there but did you ever see the room itself?"

Esther lowered her head and began to sob.

"Once. No one was around. I knew where Martin kept the key. All of the walls were covered with black curtains. There was a box on the table. It had a terrible thing in it."

"Was it a human skull?" Dalton asked quietly, already knowing the answer.

Esther looked at her in wonder.

"How did you...?" she stammered, then nodded her head. "Yes, but I don't know if it was real. There were other bones, too."

"Hands," Dalton stated. "Left and right hands. I've seen that box myself. The bones are real."

Esther buried her face in her hands.

"Now, I'm going to tell you something that might be upsetting. You've been very helpful so far and I appreciate it."

Esther looked up frightened.

"We are investigating a homicide. The victim was Alvis Hume. He was found buried on the estate. That was his skull and hands you saw in the box."

Esther fainted.

~~~

Jack wrestled with a quandary. To tell or not to tell. He sat on his deck counting the time between sets of waves. Eight seconds. They weren't large waves but restless. Something was beginning to stir at sea. He'd check the weather channel later.

Dalton seemed to be brushing him off. Zaragoza had come right out and told him to mind his own business. Yet he believed he had information that they should know about. So there it was. Should he risk being made a fool of again?

Herb Thacker was definitely involved. He lived in Topanga. Mike Eaton was last known to have gone there. Well, as far as *he* knew. Dalton and Zaragoza might have a different opinion. But there were the bones! Bat bones. And the house stank to high heaven. And the nutcase, whoever he was, acted suspiciously.

That gave him an idea. He should've thought of it before. He got up and went inside to his computer.

He had no idea that there'd be that many Herbert Thackers. After several strikeouts, he settled on one that sounded promising.

Herb Thacker. Set designer. Mendes Society. Topanga.

He next checked the Mendes Society but got nothing meaningful, or at least such that he could understand.

He'd also noticed no mention of Herb being a classic car collector. That didn't necessarily mean the guy wasn't interested in buying one. Herb could be a legitimate buyer, for all he knew.

But for sake of argument, suppose it was Herb Thatcher who'd called Mike. Gave his name as Aleister Crowley. Professed interest only in one particular car. His recently purchased XKE. Knowing what a shit Crowley was said to have been, why would he do that? Had to be another reason.

Mike was fully aware that his Jag wasn't for sale. Brenda had said Mike told Crowley, or Thacker, that he'd bring him some photographs of other available cars. Made a date for that afternoon. Next thing, Mike turns up dead. Were the pictures that bad? He had to laugh at his own joke, even though it was terrible.

No, something else was involved. But what? Then another thought occurred that wasn't the least bit funny.

Mike had been tightlipped when it came to revealing anything about his customers. Who they were. What they did. Where they lived. It was all privileged information. He was adamant. He'd die first. Well, maybe he died afterwards.

Now the question was what did they want from him that was so important they were willing to kill for it? The attempted break-in returned to his memory for another look. Nothing was taken. Obviously, whatever they wanted wasn't here.

It had to do with the car. Then it hit him.

The box containing the skull. That's what they wanted. Unfortunately, the cops had beat them to it.

He picked up his phone.

CHAPTER 30

That evening, President Richard Nixon stabbed Brian Gordon to death. The murder took place in the basement garage of Gordon's apartment building.

"I just missed him," Harold Ritter told the detective.

Sheriff Detective Andrew Furf was the lead investigator. He'd arrived on the scene thirty minutes after the deputies, who'd been the first responders. Gordon's body lay in situ next to his Porsche. The coroner was on the way.

"Just happened to be looking at the security screen when this guy wearing one of those Nixon masks ran past the parking gate," Ritter said. "I thought it was some kind of prankster. We get a lot of that."

Harold "Tex" Ritter was the doorman at the building. He was a man in his late forties who looked a little like Gary Cooper and who occasionally worked as an extra in film productions.

"What the hell was that? I said to myself," he continued. "So I went out to the front of the building. But I couldn't see anyone. It'd started to rain and was getting dark."

"Did you notice any vehicles parked on the street?" Furf asked. "He could've jumped into one."

"Yeah, but there's no parking on Doheny," Ritter smirked, as if he'd just put the kibosh on a dumb idea. "Guy could've run across the street and ducked behind a house is what I think. Could be laying low right now until things cool down, huh?"

He cocked a knowing eye at Furf.

"Was there anything about him that stood out?" the detective asked. "I mean, other than the Nixon mask."

"I didn't have a chance to really see him. Couldn't tell if he was black, white, brown or a little green man from Mars."

"How about what he was wearing, then?" Furf persisted.

"Like I said, it was getting dark," Ritter shrugged.

"All right, after you returned to the building, you went down to the garage. And that's where you discovered Mr. Gordon. How did you happen to see him? There must be lots of cars parked there."

"I didn't at first," Ritter explained. "I walked around to see if any of the cars had been broken into. Mr. Gordon was lying on the floor."

"Was he conscious?"

"No, I thought he'd had a heart attack or something. I went over to him and that's when I saw the blood and called 911."

"Does Mr. Gordon live here alone?"

"No, he lives with his wife, Dag. Actually, they were recently married."

""Do you know if she's there now? I'll need to talk with her."

"He's out of town. Mr. Dahlmgardt left for New York yesterday."

Furf smiled.

"I would like to see their apartment," he said. "I'll get a warrant. Please don't let anyone in there. Maids, maintenance people, nobody gets in, okay? In fact, I'm putting a crime scene tape across the door. Fill in your supervisor about this."

"There are four apartments on that floor. Don't know if the other people will like that."

"If they complain, have them call the Sheriffs."

Furf was notified that the coroner had arrived. He had a deputy wait with Ritter while he went back to the parking garage.

Heavy rain pelted the pavement, sending rivulets into the underground garage. Brian Gordon lay flat on his back, legs slightly spread, arms to the side. It appeared as if he'd been carefully lain down, assisted so as not to cause any discomfort. He was dressed in light grey trousers and a black blazer. A pool of blood on the cement floor at his right side glistened darkly beneath the fluorescent lights.

"See those marks on his cheeks?" the coroner pointed out. "Looks like he was grabbed from behind and a hand put across his mouth. Know more at the autopsy."

"Up close and personal," Furf said. "Must've been a knife."

"I'm going to turn him on his side."

The coroner carefully moved the body over. Furf bent down for a closer look. The back of the jacket was blood-soaked.

"Hell of a knife wound," the coroner commented. "Lower ribs. Cut right through his coat."

"Has on a nice watch," Furf said, reaching across the body and sliding his hand into the jacket's vest pocket to remove a billfold. "Couple hundred in here. Doesn't look much like robbery."

"That's evidence you're monkeying around with, detective," the coroner admonished goodheartedly.

"I know," Furf said, replacing the billfold and getting to his feet. "I'm finished here. You can bag him. Give you a call tomorrow?"

"Make it late. The ME's got a full table."

~~~

"My car's supposed to be ready tomorrow but I don't know if I can pick it up with all this rain," Jack said.

He was on the phone at home talking with Dalton. She was still at the police station. After she'd finished interviewing Esther Fillipe and having made sure the woman was well enough to be left alone, she'd had a long telephone conversation with Emilio Zaragoza. Next had come an update on Detective Rivers' progress, which fortunately was positive – he would soon be sent home where he was to remain until the doctor said differently. She might've waited for things to quiet down before returning Jack's call, except his message sounded urgent.

"That's good," she said. "Then you won't be able to do something stupid."

He hadn't told her that he'd actually been to Herb Thacker's house but had hinted that he might be on to something.

"Look, Jack, I want to be very clear about this," she said firmly. "If what you suspect has any basis of being true, then you are interfering in a police investigation. Can't you get that through your thick head? Goddamit, Jack, you can get yourself killed!"

"All right, all right, I hear you," he laughed. "It was just an idea."

"It's a dangerous idea, Jack, and it's not funny."

She sighed.

"I've spoken at length with Sheriff Zaragoza," she continued. "This is just between us, Jack, so keep it to yourself, but both the sheriff and I believe Mike Eaton's homicide is connected to Alvis Hume's. Everything is still circumstantial but we're filling in the blanks. Frankly, what you've told me does have some bearing on these deaths. That's why you have to back away from this. Both for the investigation and for your own sake. I know how you feel about Mike but let us do our job. It's that simple."

"I'll stay out of your hair," Jack said. "Although, come to think of it, you do have nice hair."

"Maybe, when this mess is over, you can introduce me to your pelicans."

"Sometimes they sleep in."

"Then it will have to be on a weekend."

"Billy Bean called," Jack said, simultaneously changing the subject and breaking the mood.

"What did he want?" Dalton asked coolly.

Billy Bean was Jack's partner in their two restaurants in Key West. Dalton had mixed feelings about the little southern town.

"New place is suffering growing pains," Jack told her. "He wanted to know when I was coming back."

"How about right away?" Dalton suggested.

"Told him I'd let him know. It's no big problem."

"I have to run, Jack. I want to get home before the rain worsens."

"Yeah, guess you'd better get out of there if it's anything like it is here. Really coming down hard now."

Jack hung up and watched the rain beat against the windows off the deck. The surf washed halfway up to his house. Probably carry away most of the beach by morning, he thought.

Later that night, a chunk of rock would loosen and fall onto Pacific Coast Highway blocking both lanes. In the wee hours, a huge slice of mountain would collapse and send a wall of mud across Interstate 5 near the Grapevine. And in Topanga, dawn would find Larry Bolt dead.

CHAPTER 31

"It's a nightmare on the five," Deputy Brinkley said. "Tell me about it," Zaragoza laughed. "Traffic stacked up all the way across the Valley. Fortunately for me, I was going in the opposite direction getting to work. Be hell to pay going home. Might just stay in town."

"Homicide in West Hollywood last night," Brinkley told him. "Furf caught it."

"Yeah?"

"Vic's name is Brian Gordon. Knifed in the back while parking his expensive Porsche. Thought you should know."

Zaragoza's jaw dropped.

"You're kidding me. Fuck!"

He grabbed up his phone.

"I've already talked with Furf," Brinkley told him. "Said you'd probably be in touch."

~~~

Sheriffs Detective Andrew Furf had made the painful telephone call. Zaragoza had given him Alison's number along with some background on her brother. Afterwards, he and Emilio met at a coffee shop in West Hollywood.

"You never know what to expect," Furf said. "People always react differently. She seemed almost resigned. Like sooner or later her brother was bound to be knocked off. Makes you wonder, huh?"

"Might be a good idea to talk with her in person," Zaragoza suggested. "I don't think she's involved anyway in her brother's death but could be she knows something that would help."

"Yeah, I'll give her a little time. I asked if they had more family. Told me there was a sister in New York she's in touch with. It's tough."

"What about Richard Nixon?" Zaragoza asked.

"Who? Oh, you mean our prime suspect," Furf laughed grimly. "Yeah, I have a deputy checking local costume shops. Could've been an old one. Those rubber masks are pretty popular. Got a mask for everybody these days."

Zaragoza debated with himself before bringing up the next subject.

"There's another person you might want to have a chat with, Andrew," he said. "Again, I wouldn't consider him a person of interest but he did know both the sister and the brother. Not only that, he's somehow mixed up in a homicide I'm working. More indirectly than being any kind of a player. His name's Jack Hunter. Lives in Malibu."

~~~

"Joyce? Where are you? Something terrible's happened to Brian."

Alison Gordon sat in her living room at home. She'd been in a near-catatonic state since receiving the news from the detective. Finally she had pulled herself together.

"I'm in New York. In fact, I just got back from Mexico," Joyce said. "You're lucky you caught me. What the hell are you talking about?"

Alison took a moment before answering.

"Brian has been murdered and I think I know who did it."

~~~

John Logan readied the body for autopsy. The ME had already made a visual examination of Brian Gordon. Before cutting into the chest, he had decided to first examine the knife wound. Gordon was turned onto his left side.

The blade had entered below the lower rib, nearly severing it. Logon leaned forward for a closer look. He'd recently seen a similar injury. He took a photograph and then an X-ray.

Satisfied, he had the body turned on its back. A headrest was placed beneath the shoulders to elevate the chest. Logan picked up the sternal saw and went about his business.

The autopsy completed and Brian Gordon returned to the morgue, Logan, now back in his office, called Detective Laura Dalton.

"A good day to you, Laura," he said. "I have something interesting for you."

"Interesting is always good. Let's hear it."

"I've just completed an autopsy on Brian Gordon."

"Wait a minute," Dalton interrupted. "I know a Brian Gordon. Not personally but by name. What happened?"

"He was stabbed to death. Don't know the circumstances but there's a similarity in the wound with that of Alvis Hume. I've compared X-rays with both. I can't say they were made by the same knife but certainly something similar. In both instances, the blade was powerfully thrust upward and twisted. Whoever did it had a great technique for killing a man."

"Where was Gordon murdered?" Dalton asked.

"West Hollywood."

"That belongs to the Sheriffs. No wonder I was in the dark. Thanks, John. I owe you."

"Yes, Laura, you do. I'll just add it to the list."

~~~

Jack answered the knock on his front door.

"Are you Mr. Hunter?" a man dressed in a snappy dark grey suit asked. "I'm Sheriffs Detective Andrew Furf."

"Hello, sir, please come in," Jack said, stepping away from the door.

"Nice place you have," Furf commented.

"Yeah, I'm lucky," Jack said. "We can talk in the living room or, if you prefer, out on the deck."

"Hell, let's go to the deck," Furf laughed. "I don't get too many chances to live the good life in Malibu."

Jack smiled.

"I wasn't always so lucky myself," he said dryly.

The weather was making up for its ugly display the night before. A clear blue sky greeted them as they stepped outside.

"Must be a bitch to have to look at this every day," Furf said.

"We privileged manage. So what was it you wanted to ask me about Brian Gordon? I didn't know him all that well."

The detective had phoned Jack and told him that he was investigating a homicide in conjunction with Zaragoza and could he come talk with him. He had deliberately failed to mention that the victim was Brian Gordon.

"When was the last time you saw Mr. Gordon?"

"Couple or three days ago. I was at his production office. Detective Zaragoza was also there."

"And that was the last time, nothing since?"

"Yeah, why?"

"You said that you didn't know Mr. Gordon all that well. What was your relationship with him?"

"None," Jack laughed. "I met him through his sister. She invited me to a party he gave at his apartment."

"Then I take it you and she have a relationship."

"No, just a casual friendship," Jack said.

"Must be more than that. She asked you to the party."

"She needed a date," Jack said.

"Why were you at Mr. Gordon's office?"

"He'd offered me a job and wanted me to meet someone."

Furf stared at Jack for a moment as he took this in.

"Let me see if I have this straight," he said. "Attractive woman you barely know asks you for a date. Man you've never met offers you a job. Does that sound funny, or is it just me?"

Jack's curse of displaying a lopsided grin came over his face.

"Guess it might sound odd," he said. "Brian found out that I used to be a producer at an ad agency. He was looking for someone to work with his director. Thought I'd be good for the job. Asked me to meet the guy. As far as Alison goes, guess I'm just lucky."

"Did you take the job?"

"No, I wasn't interested."

"Did you know Mr. Gordon was gay?"

"Yes, but what does that have to do with anything? And why all these questions about Brian Gordon?"

Jack was becoming irritated.

"I'll get to that. I assume you met his partner at the party. What did you think of him?"

"I didn't think. He seemed like a nice guy. So what?"

"Are you gay, Mr. Hunter?"

Jack let the detective wait a full minute before answering.

"Zaragoza asked me the same thing," he said calmly. "Is this the standard line of questioning for the sheriffs? No, I'm not gay."

"Brian Gordon was murdered last night."

"Jesus!" Jack said, sitting down in a deck chair.

"He was stabbed in the parking garage of his building on Doheny."

"Do you know who did it?" Jack asked. "Was it robbery or what?"

"We don't believe it was robbery nor do we have a suspect at this time," Furf said. "We are questioning everyone who might have known Mr. Gordon or had any contact with him. The reason I asked about your sexual assignment is that we are not excluding the possibility of a love triangle gone awry."

A beachcomber passed by at the water's edge. The sandy expanse had been spared by the storm.

"I can't believe that. Brian murdered? I was just talking with him the other day," Jack said in astonishment. "Have you notified his sister?"

"Yes, Miss Gordon has been told."

"There's something else you ought to know, detective."

Jack then explained the whole story, beginning with Mike Eaton's death and ending with his visit to the house in Topanga.

"That's quite a yarn," Furf said when Jack had finished. "Anything concrete to back up those claims?"

"It's no yarn, detective. No, I don't have proof of anything other than my friend is dead."

"Well, I'd best be going," he said. "Enjoy your view."

After he'd shown the detective out, Jack was now certain of one thing. He would have to finish this business himself.

~~~

"The medical examiner said that, huh. He's sure there's no mistake?"

"He's the ME of Los Angeles County" Dalton told him. "It's science, for God's sake."

She had called Emilio Zaragoza after speaking with John Logan. The fact that Brian Gordon had been stabbed had intrigued her since he was part of the crowd at the Hodges place. That and what she had learned from Esther Fellipe.

"Well, I'll be damned," Zaragoza said. "Look, I'm going call him and see if I can get a rush on that knife. Thanks, I owe you one."

"Give it to Logan. I owe him one."

She hung up and immediately thought that there was something else she'd wanted to tell him. But she couldn't think what for the life of her. It couldn't have been all that important, she rationalized.

~~~

"My sister's on her way," Alison Gordon said.

"Well, that's good," Jack told her. "When do you think she'll arrive?"

He had called Alison after Detective Furf had gone.

"Tonight. She phoned from the airport in New York. Flying directly to LAX."

"Look, if you like I can drive you there to meet her," Jack offered.

"It won't be necessary, thank you. She has a car and driver waiting."

Pretty big stuff, Jack thought to himself, feeling a little disappointed to have been so quickly dismissed.

"Okay, please let me know if there is anything I can do, Alison. I'm so sorry this has happened."

"Thank you, Jack."

~~~

The road crew had cleared the PCH of debris at Santa Monica and the highway was now clogged as usual with traffic.

""Mr. Hunter, this is Heather Williams. You car is ready."

"That's amazing," Jack said. "When can I have it?"

"Are you home?"

"Standing in my living room."

"Don't move. Klaus and I are leaving the shop right now. Be there in less than an hour with luck."

Luck didn't hold but the Jaguar XKE arrived in Malibu while there was still daylight. Heather tooted the horn as she pulled into Jack's driveway, Klaus behind her in the red MGA. It was quite a sight.

Jack had heard them drive up and had the door open.

The late afternoon light couldn't have been better for

showing off the gleaming black sports car. It'd been detailed to a tee. Even the inside walls of the tires had been conditioned. Heather jumped out of the driver's side.

"What do you think of the old thing?" she grinned.

"Is it mine?" Jack asked.

"You bet it is. We found a couple more things that needed attention in addition to those we'd talked about. Hope you don't mind."

Jack still couldn't believe this was the same car he'd given them only a few days ago. The sun even got into the act by highlighting the chrome wire wheels and trim.

"Come on in and I'll write you a check," he told them.

Once they'd gone, he could hardly wait to take the car for a spin. Hands firmly grasping the wood-rimmed steering and the top down and secured, he carefully nosed the long hood out onto the Pacific Coast Highway. And floored it.

The 4.2 inline six-cylinder engine was ready and let loose all 265 horses. He was already breaking the speed limit as he shifted into second gear. This thing was fast. And XKE speedometers didn't lie. He dropped into third and came off the throttle.

Approaching Latigo Canyon Road, he signaled and turned right into the Santa Monica Mountains. The winding canyon took him to Mulholland with its switchbacks and curves and then to Rambla Pacifico where the road dove back down to PCH, and before he knew it, he was home.

The Jag's engine ticked as it cooled in the driveway. He could smell the tire rubber and heat from the brakes. He raised the garage door and put it away for the night. There'd be another drive tomorrow.

CHAPTER 32

"Nothing I can do about it," George Overton said, yawning. "Besides, I've got a gig tonight at the club. Boys are already here."

"He's dead!" Herb Thacker cried. "Don't you understand? We have to get rid of him!"

"Your problem, son, not mine."

Herb bit his lip. He had discovered Larry Bolt's body when he'd come home that evening. Decomposition seemed to have gotten a jumpstart. He figured that might have to do with the disease. If only he'd known about those bats sooner.

"Don't be so cocky," he said. "It might be a bigger problem than you think. Larry could've given us something. He was pretty sick."

"Maybe he gave you something, sport, but not me," George chuckled. "I wasn't fucking him."

Herb laughed sarcastically.

"Cass was fucking him. We shared. Ever wonder about all those hickies?"

"You son of a bitch! What the hell are you talking about anyway?"

Larry had been feeling sick for several weeks. At first, he'd thought it was the flu. It was going around and he hadn't gotten a shot. He would just ride it out. But things had worsened. He couldn't shake the fever. Mood swings developed. Broken sleep. Larry believed demonic powers were at work. Herb had suggested a Mass of Angels.

He'd also gone on the net to see if he could match up Larry's ailments with something. By chance he'd come upon rabies. A horrible virus. That's where he'd discovered bat bites being the most common source of rabies infections in humans. That fucking mobile! And the final and most devastating part. Once you started showing the symptoms, it's already too late.

And now maybe it was too late for Herb. He had the same signs. The only question was should he warn George? He made a decision.

"I love it when you prove what a clueless bastard you are," he said. "By the way, congratulations on Brian. The mask was a nice touch."

"Here's a by-the-way for you. Cass and I are thinking of getting the hell out of Dodge. Might move back to Arizona. Or up north. You want to come along?"

"What about Mendes?"

"Leave it to the bitch."

"What would she do with it?" Herb laughed. "But you might have an idea there. Let me think on it. Right now I've got a more pressing matter."

"Don't think too long."

He went into the bedroom where Larry Bolt laid and wrapped the bedspread around him. The body was emaciated and normally would've taken little effort to carry, but in his weaken condition it was a struggle for Herb to move it out to the old Mercedes and load it in the trunk. He'd dump it in the desert tomorrow.

CHAPTER 33

Emilio Zaragoza had just come into his office when the phone rang. He set down the paper bag containing his breakfast, a cup of coffee and a bagel, on the desktop and picked up.

"Homicide. This is Sheriffs Detective Zaragoza."

"Good morning, Sheriff. John Logan here. Have some results on that knife."

Zaragoza grabbed a yellow legal pad and took out his pen.

"Yes, sir," he said excitedly. "Thank you for getting back so quickly."

"Couple of interesting things," Logan began. "The knife could have been the weapon in a murder case that's being handled by the LAPD. We found traces of human blood in the blade's locking mechanism. We were able to type it."

"Tell me about the LAPD homicide," Zaragoza said.

"Our office recently received skeletal remains that were ID'd as belonging to Alvis Hume."

"Detective Laura Dalton's case," Zaragoza broke in. "I'm familiar with that."

"Then you must know that Mr. Hume had been stabbed as well as decapitated," Logan said, somewhat annoyed at being interrupted. "May I continue?"

"Sorry. Didn't mean to jump the gun."

"LAPD has taken custody of the knife. Mr. Hume is still in residence at the morgue. I matched the knife you sent us with a wound in his back. Measurements of the blade angle and tip fit it like a glove, OJ's defense notwithstanding. As I had mentioned, we typed the blood and it's the same as Hume's."

"That's tremendous," Zaragoza said. "I'm sure Detective Dalton will be pleased."

"Wait, don't touch that dial. There's more. Your department was kind enough to send us another victim who'd been stabbed with a similar knife. And, drum roll please, the manner of the attack was identical. From behind and in the same area of the back. Upward thrust and twisting. Instant death. I have to tell you, your killer knows what he's doing."

Zaragoza was amazed. Hard to be a bad guy these days. Science will find you out every time.

"You're saying ..."

"Yes, we are saying there is a good possibility that both victims were killed by the same person," Logan finished for him. "Oh, last thing, there was only one set of prints on the knife. That includes both the handle and blade. DMV records show Overton's thumb."

This was tremendous news indeed. A breakthrough. One more piece to the puzzle with no picture. He had to sort this out.

There were three homicides that all seemed to be related to each other. Mike Eaton. Tortured and brutally burned to death in the desert. Last known to be heading to Topanga. Brian Gordon. Victim of a masked assailant. Brother of Alison Gordon. Another Topanga connection. Alvis Hume. Ex-con found headless in a grave. Los Angles this time. But somehow tied to Topanga.

Brian Gordon and Alvis Hume could be connected by the manner of their deaths. Viciously stabbed with a consistency in both technique and weapon. George Overton now being a prime suspect there. Mike Eaton's homicide seemed to be an outlier.

What about Jack Hunter? He knew Brian and Mike. And also George Overton. He fit in somewhere, too.

Hume was LAPD, the other two were his. He would

call Detective Dalton but first he needed to get hold of Andrew Furf.

Furf answered on the first ring.

"Good morning, Andrew, seems like you also got up with the chickens. Have some news that might relate to the Gordon case."

Zaragoza filled him in on what the ME had found.

"Looks like a break for LAPD," he said. "I think Overton's good for Gordon, too."

"Starting to sound like it," Furf agreed. "I've got a detail checking costume shops for that Nixon mask. I'll have them look in the knife stores, too."

"Did you talk with Jack Hunter?" Zaragoza asked.

"Yeah, I don't think he knows anything."

"Since this is LAPD's case, they'll probably want to pick up Overton. I'll give them a courtesy call."

"Okay, if LA wants to do the honors, that's fine. But I wouldn't mind tagging along."

~~~

Herb Thacker was on fire. Worse, he couldn't get out of bed. His legs didn't want to work. He'd lain there burning up with a fever since early morning.

At last, he got one foot on the floor. Then, with great effort, managed to push himself to a sitting position and finally was able to stand. Though shaky, he made his way to the bathroom and took his temperature. The thermometer read 102.5 degrees. He poured himself a glass of water but had trouble swallowing.

Now he felt cold. Wrapping himself in a blanket, he went to the living room and plopped down in an easy chair. He wouldn't be driving Larry Bolt anywhere today.

~~~

"I figured you'd want to bring him in yourself," Zaragoza said. "We're looking at him for the Brian Gordon homicide, as well. The lead detective on that would like to be present when you take Overton into custody."

He was talking with Laura Dalton. LAPD had the knife secured in the evidence room at Van Nuys and officers were ready to head out to Acton.

"We're assuming he's home," Dalton said.

"I can have a deputy drive by for a look-see," Zaragoza told her.

"If you don't think it will spook him, fine," Dalton said. "Why don't I hook up with your detective near the location and we all go from there?"

Zaragoza gave her the name of the restaurant in Acton and let her know that traffic was good now that the 5 had cleared.

That business taken care of, he picked up his cup of coffee. It was cold. He grabbed out his earlier phone messages from the in-box. Nothing pending that he needed to concern himself with.

Except for the one left by Jack Hunter giving the address of Aleister Crowley in Topanga. Jack had mentioned that he was going there this morning.

~~~

Jack pulled the XKE into the tiny shopping mall and parked in front of Xanadu Books. To his disappointment a closed sign was stuck in the window. He got out of the car and peered inside the darkened store. No sign of anyone being there. Too bad, he'd wanted to talk with Alison Gordon first.

He walked to the coffee shop a few doors down in hope of finding her. No luck. Nothing else to do but go ahead. Like he'd said, he'd have to finish this himself.

CHAPTER 34

The FedEx delivery truck stopped on the side of the road by the old wooden wagon. It's driver hopped out with a package in her arms and walked up the driveway toward the house. A double-cab pickup truck waited in front where it was being loaded with household items.

"FedEx!" the delivery woman shouted through the open door.

George Overton came outside.

"What the hell do you want?" he grumbled.

"Have a package for you, sir," she said with a Southern drawl.

She was an attractive woman who looked like she took care of herself. This wasn't lost on George.

"Package, huh?" he grinned, eyeing her. "Who'd be sending me anything?"

"Are you George Overton?" she asked.

"Yeah, that's me. What's your name, honey?"

"Joyce," she smiled tightly.

George's grin broadened, accompanied by a leer.

"You must have a secret admirer," Joyce said with a wink. "Good-looking fellow like you, why, I wouldn't be surprised if you had to beat the ladies off with a stick."

"Like the fella said, big dogs is always licking my hand," he leaned to her and whispered.

"You're so bad," she teased with a girly laugh.

Cass appeared in the doorway.

"George, better get this stuff loaded," she sniffled. "I don't feel so good. Think I've got the flu."

George shot her an angry look.

"Where do I sign?" he asked, taking the package from the woman.

"Doesn't require a signature, hon. Hope your cold gets better, ma'am."

She waved to Cass and walked hurriedly back to her truck.

~~~

Dalton introduced herself to Andrew Furf, who was waiting in the restaurant parking lot. She'd driven her Porsche. An LAPD patrol car with two officers for backup had led the way with the roof rack blazing.

"Good to meet you, Detective Furf. You can ride with me or I can go with you."

"I'll go with you," Furf smiled. "Never ridden in one of these little things."

"How far is the house from here?" Dalton asked.

"About ten minutes or so. I swung by on my way here. His truck's in the yard, so there's a good chance he's there."

~~~

"Aren't you going to open it?" Cass asked excitedly.

"Hold your horses," George told her. "Let me get my knife out. Thing's taped up all to hell."

Cass crowded closer for a better look. George cut through the tape and ripped off the cardboard top. Inside was a black metal camera box, a cubic foot in size and with a key taped to its top.

"Well, I'll be damned," he said, removing the box and setting it on a side table by the door.

George removed the key, inserted it in the slot on the front of the box and turned it, detonating two pounds of Semtex plastic explosive that had been shaped for maximum blast effect.

~~~

"That's it ahead," Andrew Furf pointed. "Just the other side of that wooded lot."

His cellphone rang.

"Furf," he answered. "Oh, hi, Emilio, we're coming up on the house right now. What do you need?"

He paused while Zaragoza spoke.

"Emilio wants to know if Jack Hunter called you about a Topanga address," he said to Dalton.

"Haven't checked my messages," she said.

Furf told Zaragoza and ended the call.

"What did he say?" Dalton asked.

"Something I can't repeat to a lady."

The force of the explosion nearly caused Dalton to lose control of the car. A huge fireball shot into the sky and was swallowed by a billowing plume of smoke. She pulled off the road, narrowly missing a ditch, and stopped.

"Duck!" she yelled to Furf, covering her head with her hands and scooting down in the seat. Debris began to pepper them.

"Holly shit!" Furf said, trying to get below the dash.

The patrol car had jinked to the opposite of the road and gone into a shallow ditch. It was taking the brunt of the bombardment. A larger piece of something smashed its windshield.

When the smoke cleared, little remained of where the house once stood. Small flames licked nervously around the site. The pickup truck, a crumpled mass, rested in the center of the road.

Furf got his wits together enough to call 911. Dalton ran over to the patrol car to check on her officers.

~~~

The FedEx truck turned onto a dirt road off Sand Canyon, drove down about a hundred yards and stopped. It was a remote and barren area near a state park. The woman got out and opened the rear doors. Inside was a green Kawasaki Ninja motorcycle.

She undressed, exchanging the delivery driver's uniform for a pair of jeans and a black leather jacket. Then she tucked up her hair and put on a full-face helmet and gloves. The bike was rolled off the back of the truck, started, and left idling on its kickstand. Back in the truck, she set the timer on an incendiary device strapped to the side of a two-gallon plastic gasoline container, got out and shut the doors. She had sixty seconds. She was on the main road heading for Route 14 when the truck burst into flames.

~~~

Jack parked the XKE behind the old Mercedes in the drive. It was the only thing around that indicated someone might be at home. Even the birds were silent. He got a whiff of something foul as he walked past the car to the front door.

"Hello," he shouted, giving the door a couple of raps. "Anybody there?"

This wasn't a good idea, he thought as he waited. He should've left it to the sheriff or Laura. He knocked again and heard some shuffling inside.

"I'm coming," a weak voice called. The door opened. Herb Thacker stood wrapped in his blanket. "Yeah?"

"Hi, Herb. I'm here with the car you wanted. May I come in?"

Jack expected the door to be slammed in his face, but surprisingly Herb motioned him in.

"Excuse the mess," Herb apologized with a wave. "Sit anywhere you like."

He returned to the easy chair. Jack took a seat in a kitchen chair across the room from him. The place still had a foulness about it but was not as suffocating as on his last visit.

"What was that about my car?" Herb asked bewilderedly. The corners of his mouth glistened.

"The Jaguar you asked Mike Eaton about," Jack said. "Remember? You wanted to buy it. He came here to show you some others."

Herb shook his head, then his eyes brightened.

"Oh, Mike," he said with a smile. "He was a funny guy."

Jack edged forward in his chair. Herb had just admitted to Mike Eaton having been at the house.

"I met your friend the last time I was here," Jack said. "Is he around?"

"You must mean Larry. He's waiting in the car."

Jack involuntarily shuddered. He hadn't noticed anyone in the car. But that smell ....

"What's your name?" Herb asked, squinting as if to see better.

"Jack Hunter. I think you might have visited me one night, Herb. I saw your Mercedes in my driveway."

"If you say so, guess I did. Shit, it's hot in here. You warm, Jack?"

"I'll open the door," Jack offered.

"That's a little better," Herb said when Jack had returned to his chair. "As long as those fucking birds don't come in. They're pissed off at me. So what was it you wanted to know?"

"Tell me about Mike. You said he was a funny guy."

"George also thought he was funny. George wants to give Mendes to the bitch, you know," he added offhandedly. "But she won't take it."

Herb's head dropped down on his chin. Jack thought he'd passed out. Suddenly, he jerked up.

"I married them," he pronounced. "Martin and the bitch. Nice wedding. Baptized them both in salt water."

Jack was confused.

"I'm not sure I understand, Herb. Who did you marry?"

"Martin Hodges and Alison Gordon," he snapped. "What's so hard to understand? George wasn't in favor. He hated Brian, especially after the accident."

Herb began to rock back and forth in his chair.

"They were racing their cars, Brian and Martin," he said. "George believes it was Brian's fault that Martin was killed."

"That was the accident on the Pacific Coast Highway?" Jack asked.

"But George got even with Brian," Herb said. "That's George for you."

~~~

Zaragoza turned off Topanga Canyon Road and headed up the mountain.

"Check these house numbers," he said to Deputy Brinkley. "Some of them are missing."

"Think we've got a little farther to go," Brinkley said.

He had grabbed the deputy as he was leaving the station. Neither was aware of the events in Acton at the time.

"Here it is on the right," Brinkley called out. "Where that black sports car's parked."

~~~

"Everyone took part in the sacrifices," Herb said. "It was a ceremony, you see."

"Including Alison?"

"No, the bitch didn't have the stomach," he laughed cruelly. "She wasn't really one of us, when you came down to it. Martin kept her on. Made her a priestess. Can you believe that?"

"These sacrifices ... they were animals, right?"

"Not always, sometimes we used people. That would be a very special occasion, of course. Usually, a homeless person would be taken. Young boys were preferred. No one missed them."

Jack had become disgusted and had heard enough. Alison had lied. For what reason, he couldn't guess. To protect him? Everything was an illusion. But he had to ask.

"Did Alison know about the human sacrifices?"

"Not unless her lovely brother told her."

"Tell me what happened to Mike Eaton." he demanded sharply.

Herb smacked his lips.

"So damn thirsty," he rasped. "Mike Eaton, you said? Obstinate old fucker. There's a forget-me-not from him in the refrigerator, if you want."

Jack got up and ran over to open the door.

"You son-of-a-bitch!" he said angrily and spun around to find Herb Thacker on his feet and pointing a .44 revolver at him.

"Move over by that window," Herb ordered, wavering slightly.

~~~

Zaragoza parked the Land Rover on the side of the road about fifty feet beyond the house.

"The front door looked like it was open," Brinkley said. "Somebody's there."

They crept silently up to the house.

"You smell that?" Zaragoza whispered as they walked past the Mercedes.

"Yeah, think we better check it out after this."

They approached the front door, keeping to its left side, Zaragoza in the lead.

~~~

"We sent him straight to hell," Herb cackled. "Then we all went back to George's and partied."

"Was he still alive when you did that?" Jack asked coldly.

"Of course, that was the whole point, you ignoramus," Herb told him. "Mike was our gift to Lucifer."

Jack shifted, taking in the room, hoping to spot something he could use as a weapon. He saw a shadow at the door. Someone was standing there.

~~~

"There are two of them," Brinkley whispered.

Both officers had their guns out.

"One sounded like Jack Hunter," Zaragoza said. "Ready?"

Zaragoza banged open the screen door.

"Sheriffs!" he shouted. "Get on the floor!"

Herb swung around toward them, the revolver in hand.

"He's got a gun!" Jack yelled, grabbing the bat skeleton mobile dangling next to him from the ceiling and hurling it at Herb.

The collection of sharp little bones struck Herb in the face, entangling itself in his hair. He fired wildly.

Brinkley felt the sting of the bullet as it creased his neck.

"Goddamit!" he said, slapping at the wound.

Zaragoza got off two quick rounds before Herb could cock the old single-action revolver for another shot. Herb sank to the floor dead.

The detective walked slowly to where the body lay and kicked the gun aside. Then he turned around to his deputy.

"You okay, Charles?"

"Just a scratch," he said, examining the blood on his hand and looking pale enough that he might faint.

Jack had hit the deck when he'd thrown the mobile. He remained there not daring to move a muscle.

"What about you, Mr. Hunter?" Zaragoza asked.

"Okay if I get up now?" Jack answered.

ONE MONTH LATER

Jack turned off US 1 and drove up the short grade to the parking lot at Nepenthe. It was a calendar-picture day in Big Sur and good weather had followed him all the way from Malibu.

The restaurant there sat on the side of a mountain a few hundred feet above the Pacific Ocean. Not only did it offer one of the best views on the West Coast, the whole place was locked in time. The clock had stopped running in the sixties.

Jack walked out on the patio and ordered a cup of coffee and a breakfast roll.

He'd gotten away at six o'clock that morning, driving north on the 101 until Morro Bay, where he'd cut over to Route 1. The road from there up to the Monterey Peninsula had been carved from the mountains with the Jaguar XKE in mind. Of course, back then they didn't have RVs to worry about. He'd been stuck behind one or more since San Simeon. Still, it had been a good run for the car.

He took his coffee to a vacant table. The ocean, blue and calm as its namesake, stretched across the broad horizon.

Events of late had been quite a run for him, too. He'd lost a friend. Nearly lost another. Almost lost his own life.

Laura Dalton had escaped serious injury from the explosion, shattered nerves notwithstanding. Her car hadn't fared as well. He had put her in touch with Heather, who gave the little Porsche a factory-perfect paint job. On the quiet, he'd asked her to do whatever was necessary to the rest of the car. He took care of those expenses.

No trace was found of George Overton and Cass in the remains of their house, although a cadaver dog did signal in one small area.

Mike Eaton was buried in Forest Lawn. His son made it to the funeral.

After the shootout at Herb Thacker's, Jack had filled in Emilio Zaragoza on everything he'd learned that morning. They found Larry Bolt's body in the Mercedes. Later, two more unidentified bodies had been discovered on the property. Mike's finger was taken as evidence, which pretty much closed the case for the Sheriffs.

There'd been a major uproar after the medical examiner had discovered the rabies virus in Bolt and Thacker. Demands were made with dire warnings that everyone involved be treated. Since he'd never had any close contact with either man, Jack had opted out. So had Zaragoza. Brinkley, who had been superficially wounded in the incident and could have been contaminated along with the medical technicians who'd picked up the bodies, went for the vaccine.

One puzzling incident was the discovery of a burned-out FedEx truck on a state park fire road near Acton. The VIN number showed the truck had been reported stolen but little was left of the interior.

Xanadu was for sale. All the books had been cleared out. Also, Alison Gordon's house in the canyon had been put on the market. Jack hadn't mentioned her having belonged to the Satanist group when he'd talked with Zaragoza. He really didn't believe that she'd had anything to do with the deaths. At any rate, now she seemed to have disappeared into thin air.

Herb Thacker's chilling account of the homeless victims in the ritualistic murders had gotten to him. He had once been homeless himself. It is a period of disillusion that no one should have to go through. He had determined that he would make a small effort against that condition for those poor souls unfortunate enough to experience it. And the knew where that effort would take place.

He got up from the table. Took a last look at the splendid view. And walked to the parking lot.

~~~

Monterey was less than an hour's drive from Big Sur. He detoured through the charming little town of Carmel, which was right next door.

Eric Nystrom was in his office finishing up lunch when Jack drove up in the XKE.

"Nice," he commented, stepping outside.

"Runs as good as it looks," Jack grinned.

Eric walked around the car giving it the once and twice over.

"Sure you want to do this?" he asked.

"Couldn't be more sure. Got the pink slip right here."

Odd about the Jaguar. It had begun as a dream only to end as a nightmare. Once important to him and now not at all.

Jack handed him a large envelope containing the car's registration and other documents.

"The auctions during the Pebble Beach concourse have had big turnouts the last couple of years," Eric said. "Probably do well there. XKEs are going through the roof."

"Whatever you think is best," Jack said.

"There's another option," Eric offered. "I have three people right now who'd buy your car in a minute."

Jack considered this.

"How about having them bid on it?" he suggested. "It's all for a good cause."

"Let's give it a try," Eric agreed. "And just to be sure, the money goes to homeless shelters, right?"

"Yeah, there's a list of them in the envelope. Send the check to my lawyer after you take out your commission."

"Oh, I won't be taking anything," Eric smiled. "After

all, it's for a good cause."

He put out his hand and Jack shook it.

"One thing you could do," Jack said. "How driving me to the airport in the Jag?"

~~~

Jack looked out the window of the commuter jet at 26,000 feet as the Central Coast inched by below. He'd be on the redeye to Atlanta tonight and in Key West by midday tomorrow.

Right now, and maybe forever, that was where he belonged. It'd taken this sojourn to the West Coast to show his mind what, if he were honest, his heart already knew. He longed to feel the moist heat on his skin and breathe in the scent of pungent flora.

Morro Bay and its landmark rock came into view. He'd passed there going the other way earlier today. He thought of all the roads through life he had traveled and wondered about those yet to come.

There was California Route 1 snaking up the coast. A highway carved from the mountains that had carried him to both an ending and a beginning.

He motioned to the flight attendant who was serving coffee. Then, a final glance at Route 1.

One was not an evil number.

Thank you for reading.
Please review this book. Reviews help others find
Absolutely Amazing eBooks and inspire us to keep
providing these marvelous tales.

If you would like to be put on our email list to receive
updates on new releases, contests, and promotions, please
go to AbsolutelyAmazingEbooks.com and sign up.

ACKNOWLEDGEMENT

Once more, my thanks goes to my wife, Laura, who put up with the dropped words, incorrect tenses, misspellings and colloquialisms while editing the manuscript. Also, many thanks for her story suggestions along the way. Thanks, Laura.

ABOUT THE AUTHOR

Robert Coburn is originally from Norfolk, Virginia. After high school in Norfolk, he spent three years in the US Army as a helicopter crew chief stationed in Berlin, Germany. He returned home to attend college at Richmond Professional Institute (Now VCU) in Richmond, Virginia, where he earned a Bachelor of Science degree in Advertising. He also met his wife in Richmond while a student there.

Coburn has worked at major advertising agencies in New York and Los Angeles. His ads have won top awards both nationally and internationally. He is an instrument rated commercial pilot and plays saxophone. He and his wife now live in Carmel, California.

ABSOLUTELY AMAZING eBOOKS

AbsolutelyAmazingEbooks.com or

AA-eBooks.com

Made in the USA
San Bernardino, CA
30 January 2016